DYSTOPOLIS

Christopher J. Fraser

Also by Christopher J. Fraser

Tales From The End

Published by Hiatus Press

1

ISBN 978-0-9561519-5-7

www.chrisjfraser.com

For Arden.

AN IMPROVISED JIGSAW

Everything is a muffled echo.

The dull, metallic thud of footsteps suddenly stops. You have your cot, your toys. Safety. There are hushed voices outside, one calm, one with a sense of urgency. You blink to refresh the bulletin, and switch back to your music in one synaptic flicker. The thin antenna fused to your temple provides you with all the information you could ever want. Even now, as you try and make out what those two unfamiliar voices are saying, there are houses being built, skyscrapers under construction, and a whole new civilization rushing up into existence - a great, mechanical organism that never stops. Sector by sector, the decomposing waste of centuries past is being brutally rinsed away to make way for something new.

You are eleven years old, and live in one of thousands of underground pods across the city. The people outside have come to tell your future.

They enter. Both wear dark suits and glasses. One - a woman - stands by the door, eyes scanning back and forth, checking an array of screens only she can see. She looks anxious to move on. The other slowly pulls up a seat, takes your hand in his, and has the sort of vocal intonation that instantly lulls you into feeling secure. You've never met him before, but the moment you make eye contact, trust feels inevitable.

"Tim Reitman, eighteen years old, steps out of his room, turns right, and sees a long spiral staircase at the end of the corridor, winding upwards. His curiosity has gotten the better of him. Even though Timothy is not a curious boy by his nature, preferring instead the simple comforts of a warm home and a clear set of responsibilities, he climbs the stairs because he really believes that he can find that sense of security when he reaches the top." You blink slowly. Tim Reitman is your name, but you're eleven, not eighteen. What's more, you've seen the staircase at the end of the hallway, and it scares you. Still, you stay there, transfixed, feeling utterly pliable. There's something about the man's voice that keeps you comfortable. It makes you feel like you're sinking into your mattress. Like the whole room is slowly, gently wrapping its arms around you.

"When he reaches the top, Tim checks the map on his specs, and heads for the headquarters of the city Watch. He's always wanted to be a watch officer - the kind he sees in flicks, locking up bad guys and keeping people safe. Everyone is so good down those stairs that there's no need to keep watch for that sort of thing, but up on the surface, he wants to make things stay just as calm and orderly as when he was a kid.

He immediately gets the job. Within days, he realizes he

was *born* to do this. His apartment is cozy. His cops and robbers figurines sit by his bed, finally ignored in favor of the real thing. One day, Tim brings home a girl from work, and he wants her to stay with him - not just the night, but permanently. And just like that, Tim lives happily ever after."

There's a weird silence. The man telling the story looks straight into your eyes, looking for something. Eventually, he finds it, smiles, rests a paternal hand on your shoulder, and leaves your room.

Seven years later, so do you.

*

"Any trouble tonight, James?"

Hundreds of kilometers of wasteland lay below. Squinting hard enough, one could make out the occasional speck of light - fires lit by savages, far away, too distant to be even reported as a low-level threat. Stopfordia was a city designed to be self-contained - there were no walls, but no-one stood a chance once they got past the threatening, dust-bitten signs at the side of the road. Next to the two men was a great, hulking turret scanning the horizon for approaching threats. It was important to keep any unknown variables out.

James - Tim had never bothered to find out his full name - laughed and shook his head, lighting up a cigarette. Being on the night watch got lonelier the further out of the central district he got, so Tim made a point of visiting each border guard before he finished for the night. He preferred the bustle of the leisure complex, a moderated kind of keeping the peace, where no street was ever dark enough to encourage the ugliest impulses. Tonight, he had helped split up a bar brawl and guided a few lost souls to the metro, but otherwise served as a deterrent - just another uniform on the streets. That last part was important. Everything in its proper place was the idea, but people sometimes forgot to keep to the path prescribed for them. He was one of the many ensuring they did.

With the dawn came the rain. Once, long ago, people had been slaves to the weather. It seemed bizarre, meaningless even - lives cut short by tsunamis, entire swathes of continents rendered uninhabitable simply by virtue of the temperature: total chaos. People had tried to ascribe meaning to it all - the workings of some shadowy organization called God, who worked in ways so mysterious that no-one could even guess at their intentions - but it was still hard to understand why anyone could bear to live in such a world. There was a theory that the weather had been the first thing to drive the ancestors underground.

This rain was planned. It was a brief shower, designed to refresh those on their morning commute, and drive indoors the reveling stragglers from the night. It made Tim's job easier - so many were already hurrying indoors that the streets would be virtually empty.

Tim stepped into the watchtower elevator and watched the ground rush towards him. He lived only a few blocks away, in the apartment that had come with the job ten years ago. It remained essentially unchanged - a slightly friendlier virtual interface, the occasional customized wallpaper, but it was a home designed to suit him. Small, warm, serene. Not too claustrophobic, but neither was it spartan. Exactly the sort of place where he could unwind after a night on his feet.

As he settled into bed, the outside bustle of the morning commuters slowly lulled him to sleep.

Everyone knew that the secret to a meaningful life was to see it as a story. A boy, with the same humble beginnings as everyone else, might one day emerge to become an upstanding member of society, defending the law and facilitating the happiness and safety of everyone else. One day soon, he might meet someone, start a family, and proudly watch them grow up. Decades in the future, he might close his eyes for the last time, a smile on his face, satisfied in the knowledge that the legacy he was leaving behind was a safe city, a loving family, all while staying strictly within the confines of a very reasonable comfort zone. The perfect happy ending. He gradually slipped into unconsciousness. Another night over. A tiny progression through a brilliantly unremarkable second act.

Six hours later, he was woken by his specs, pulsing an alarm through the haze of sleep. It was the same voice as usual - the neutral female VI he had chosen during his first week - but the code she was announcing made his blood run cold: 1-8-7, E_5C_3. E_5C_3 was shorthand for Warwick Towers, his own apartment building - that alone was unremarkable. The number, though - he hadn't heard it spoken before, but he knew what it meant. The homicide division had been dissolved, with the understanding that the number of murders subject to investigation was far too low to require a whole workforce. In the highly unlikely event that there ever *was* one, official policy was that the closest to the scene would pick up the job. It meant that everyone was on standby for something that would never happen. Something that would never happen had happened a couple of floors above him while he slept. For a moment, Tim felt his lower lip tremble.

He scrambled out of bed.

The body lay sprawled in the doorway to her apartment. It took a moment for Tim to realize that he knew her - or, at least, had passed her regularly on the way to work. She had been the victim of countless awkward smiles and elevator silences, and now she was the victim of blunt force trauma to the back of her fragile skull. He felt numb. Seeing photographs of bodies - even seeing them laid out in the morgue - didn't prepare you for a crime scene. He could feel each section of his brain slipping into shutdown. His vision blurred, and he could feel his heart thumping in his ears.

There was a job to do, but the usual confidence and initiative didn't come. She was pretty - young, probably recently sent above ground. Her black hoodie and grey jeans betrayed no bloodstains, but the back of her head - crumpled tissue paper leaking red ink - left nothing to the imagination.

He was vaguely aware of other officers arriving at the scene, but they were blurs in his periphery as the tunnel vision set in. Collapsing to the floor, the last thing he saw before blacking out was her cold, dead stare.

*

"Afternoon, Tim. Take a seat."

Tim's boss was sat exactly as expected. He was reclining so far back in his custom-made leather chair that he looked like he could slide off at any second, suspenders hanging loosely off his stick-insect frame, his face thin but constantly flushed. He was an odd-looking man, all tousled brown hair and wrinkles in areas of his face where you wouldn't expect them, but no-one ever doubted that he was in the right place. He was tall enough, and spoke in a grumbling baritone - enough to command authority, but only in a division with so little activity. Next to the Chief Liaisons, he looked pathetic, but as a friendly face whose role was to reassure the public, everyone agreed that Detective Chief Inspector Mikael Simms of the Stopfordia Night Watch Unit probably *shouldn't* look too imposing.

6

This was his fifth performance review with his boss, and the first Tim had been to since the beginning of his therapy regime. The anxiety attacks - flashes of blood across mundane moments, a crescendo of creeping horror - had subsided after a month or so, but he would still wake up occasionally with the same afterimage lingering. Things like this happened, of course. No society with an obsessively keen interest in the inner lives of its citizens could ever let any mental state fall too sharply. Not without good reason - whatever those reasons might be. Maybe, for some, madness was its own reward.

Tim saw very little of his boss. As one of the few dozen citywide night officers, he spent very little time in the office, signing in to work via his specs at dusk and logging out at dawn, only meeting colleagues during his midnight breaks and if he happened to bump into them during the course of his duties. The Night Watch liked to keep its officers' boots on the ground, and Simms stood out as an exception to the rule - Simms was a man of paperwork, keeping tabs on everyone from the comfort of his office. He always arrived earlier and left later, giving the impression that he never left the building. Usually, he was just a shadow in a tinted window, seven stories up, peering down at the officers patrolling the area.

Tim sat on the couch opposite the desk, and smiled weakly over at Simms. The office was styled to be as accommodating as possible - when the inspector had arrived, he'd specifically asked for a chair that put him at the same height as his staff, and had nearly succeeded in getting rid of the desk separating him from employees. It was commonly known (or maybe assumed) that his slouched demeanor was less a mark of laziness, and more to make some concession for his absurd height. It was as if Simms was consumed by the need to be at eye level with people, but his genetics were conspiring against him.

A sigh escaped Tim's mouth as Simms looked at him expectantly. "I suppose you want to know if I've fully recovered."

"Now, Tim. You know you're not here to be challenged - I just thought that it was time for another chat." Tim relaxed his shoulders a little. Approaching this from a friendly angle might well work - even the chief, anti-social from a mile off, needed people around him to stay sane. There were enough staff in the department to keep the man feeling social, but when he went home it was invariably alone. Tim found himself thinking about inner lives again. He had been in a couple of happy, if brief relationships, but Simms was all of sixty years old and unattached. He softened his expression, and returned the gaze.

"Really? Even I can see that what I did - what happened to me - wasn't exactly professio-" Simms waved off the end of his sentence and suddenly jumped to his feet. He beckoned Tim over to the window, pointing off into the distance with his bony fingers. "There," he murmured pensively, "just on the horizon. Can you see it?" Tim squinted. The fog was a little thick today, but he could make out a vague shape of a half-constructed tower, new to the skyline. "You'll never guess what they're building."

Tim turned to him. "Things are being built all the time. You should know - I've seen three buildings just like that rise up out of the ground since you started here."

Simms looked animated. The chief's face was the sort that could never look bored, each little crevice and laughter line creasing up at even the hint of an opportunity. "They're relocating CAIN, Tim. Just think of it. It'll be the first time they're taking it above ground."

It was obvious why he was excited. The Central Artificial Intelligence Network, to all intents and purposes, housed the government. In the two hundred years of waiting underground, a strategy had been devised by the founders to study everything they could about humanity, to make everything *fit* when the world's population finally resurfaced. Simms had been a subject for half his life, emerging after decades of analysis. CAIN, developed over decades, was the world's most advanced psychotherapist and cultural architect, with a mind-bogglingly deep knowledge of everything from business practices to sexual politics, and it was semi-autonomous even now - learning and adapting to every outcome with minimal oversight from the best and brightest. It was society's biggest failsafe against another catastrophe, so tuned in to the nuances and idiosyncrasies of every citizen that hardly anyone would ever go rogue. It was nicknamed The Narrative Strategy, thanks to its uncanny ability to plan lives so they just made *sense*.

There was a reason the homicide division was non-existent, and it was that even an act as extreme as murder was always sanctioned by CAIN; premature deaths were always part of the plan, never subject to investigation unless there was some role the Watch was supposed to play. From an outside perspective - and this is what Tim was still battling with - what might seem like a meaningless killing in cold blood would make sense if you were in possession of all the pieces. Ordinarily, whatever that woman's life had been before she was bludgeoned to death, her murder would have been calculated as a meaningful, natural ending, and her killer would be known already - CAIN had assassins who lived outside the formal law of the Watch, and any deaths at their hands were never investigated. That the Watch knew at all might be for any reason. Perhaps there was a need for a higher percentile of social fear in response to the public inquiry. Maybe the culprit needed prison to carry his narrative arc into the next act, or maybe imprisonment was his endgame. These things weren't questioned - the Watch just took on any case that was handed to them.

They were usually there for the fringe elements - minor aberrations, rarely anything that could alter someone's path. The laws of the Watch were a secondary framework, designed to keep things running smoothly with very little nuance. It was rare that they were required to facilitate CAIN's machinations directly, but not unheard of. It just hadn't been this gruesome for a while.

You were free to ignore the advice of CAIN, but if you did and things went wrong, you had no safety net. Create a mess after following CAIN's rules, chances are you'd get a quick reprimand and a small pay cut at the most - a deterrent, but nothing more. If you did the same after ignoring the strategy, the consequences didn't bear thinking about. But no-one did. It was common wisdom that acting out of character was seen as an error - most could fall into the margins, but some errors were too big to reprogram - those whose ripples went too far.

Over the last month, his therapist had been reminding him that The Narrative Strategy was a good thing. It had given Tim exactly the sort of job he'd always wanted - one where he could spend most of his days outside, where he'd get the immense feeling of satisfaction from seeing an angry parking violator soften and smile after a quick conversation, where he could have an active social life with a couple of colleagues. His job fit his personality perfectly. Even the events of a month ago were more palatable if you accepted that there was likely a valid reason for them, no matter how obfuscated it might be.

Tim got up and stood by the window.

"Won't they have to take it offline?" he asked. Simms furrowed his brow. Clearly, he hadn't considered this.

"I expect so. Of course - heh - we were never told, but as far as I can tell it currently exists as a clustered underground series of systems, spread out over a thousand square miles or so. They'll probably transfer each sector one by one. Minimize disruption, you know. But Tim, isn't this *exciting*? Every time something from below reappears up here, I can't help getting enthusiastic - it's just wonderful. But you're young; I'd imagine it's not quite the same for you."

"I'm not *that* young. You might need that attitude for your grandkids, but I can still recognize when something's a big deal." As soon as he said it, Tim regretted mentioning the idea of Simms having grandchildren. That was pretty unlikely.

If he was bothered, he didn't let it show. "You're right. No sense in patronizing you. But there we are... thirty-three years, and CAIN's finally coming up for air. You know, I remember reading about government buildings having such *prestige*... oh, I wonder. Back before all of this, centuries ago, there were grand arenas, elaborate, domed, marble mansions, so many monuments to *decadence*. I imagine we'll get there someday, but right now it's all a bit..." He wrinkled his nose. "Functional. Are you up on your architecture, Tim?"

Tim grinned, and squinted again. "Not in the slightest." Simms raised his eyebrows.

"A shame. I don't know... maybe I'm just a romantic, but I really think this could be a valuable reminder of our significance...."

He seemed to be half-lost in introspection. Time to leave. Tim stood up, offered his hand, and replied. "I'm sure any attempt to move above ground is a good thing, sir. Is it okay if I...." he trailed off. "Go" felt a bit abrupt.

It took Simms a second to notice Tim standing there. "What? Oh. Sorry, Tim, don't mind me. Keep doing what you do best." He took the outstretched hand, shook it absent-mindedly, and turned back to the window as Tim left.

Tim walked out of the room in a daze. Interactions with other people - the people he was supposed to feel familiar with, at least - had become fuzzier, like peering through static. He could still do his job as effectively as before, but the prospect of his nightly social calls to the guard towers filled him with dread. He got through them by switching to autopilot, refusing to engage emotionally. There had been the sparks of a potential relationship with a staffer at the Watch HQ before, but it had all but fizzled out. All normal, of course. Dissociation was a blank canvas upon which to begin the healing process. Or something.

The fact that everything was under control only got him so far. CAIN's sometimes-fatal reach was common knowledge, but one rarely saw the darker ends that people met. The advice that it gave was so often benign - take this job, start this class, make love to this person - that the fact that there was nearly a 100% acceptance rate was hardly a surprise, but the idea that the strategy could suggest someone's premature death and still deem it important seemed somehow askew - not adorned with the usual positive reinforcement. Despite the constant reassurances from the people around him, Tim had the nagging feeling that he had seen something he wasn't supposed to.

He shook his head. No. He knew that feeling came from himself. The variance here was in Tim's own psychological state, as he had been reminded time and time again. Actions were always accounted for, but minds were harder. There was a reason he was being treated: because the sooner he felt well, the sooner that CAIN could operate at its usual efficiency. He just needed to be fixed.

That thought brought him some reassurance. He felt safer. He cast one look back at the chief's office before stepping into the elevator. Simms was still standing by the window, unmoving. His tall, gaunt frame was a silhouette against a dazzling sunset. It was time to go to work.

That night, there was another murder. He wasn't called to the scene, but it didn't stop the flashbacks from being triggered.

The details came through in the late night report from HQ, just as he had finished sending over a ticket to a group of revelers who had broken the noise barrier. As they moved off, arm in arm, now speaking in stage whispers and giggles, the item flew into the periphery of his specs. 1-8-7, C2A1. The Burnage Apartments. A thirty-seven-year-old male had been found in the doorway of his home, bludgeoned to death with a blunt instrument from behind. There were no immediately apparent connections - personal, financial, professional - between this victim and the one Tim had witnessed, apart from the method. This thought did not reassure him.

He blinked. A surge of anger rose up - not at the futility of the crime, but that it was being reported to him at all. During his recovery, all violent crimes were supposed to be blacklisted and filtered out of any reports he received. His hands were already shaking. He dismissed the message angrily. Someone else would deal with it.

He wandered to the perimeter, an hour early. He hadn't visited James in a fortnight. His breaks had recently been consumed by allowing his mind to breathe, but right now all he wanted was to vent.

"You alright, Tim? Haven't seen you in a while. You look stressed."

"Yeah. You get it?" James looked nonplussed. Tim sighed impatiently. "The latest report from HQ, James. You see it?" The confusion turned to bemusement.

"Of course, Tim. It's hard to avoid."

Tim's face screwed up. "You don't think it's a bit twisted, the admin staff feeding me reports on homicides? You must have seen the details." James put up a hand to stop him.

"Hold on. What are you talking about? I never saw anything about another murder. A couple of robberies, sure."

Tim sighed. "You must have missed it. Scan back to about 4:32am." He watched as James scrolled back, looking keenly, shaking his head.

"Nothing. Are you feeling alright?"

It was as if time had skipped a beat - everything was suddenly cold, alien, out of sync. He stood back and nearly tripped over his own feet, scrolling back to four, then three in the morning, where there was nothing.

"I...." He was excruciatingly aware of each breath, terrified that if he didn't force out the next he would be breathing his last. The elevator was only a few meters away, but stumbling over to it took a century. James was staring at him. Tim attempted a reassuring smile, but what appeared on his face was so grotesque that he was sure it had only made things worse.

The ground crept closer. The moment he was out of view of everyone, he began to hyperventilate. The words of the report repeated again and again in his mind, gaining in intensity until everything else was blocked out. It was as if the act of forgetting could transform a death into a delusion.

On his notebook he scrawled every detail he could remember, and got into bed, his eyes locked open, unable to stop the noise in his own head. It was only by the approach of midday, when the traffic outside peaked and the light shone into his bedroom the brightest, that the terror gave way to something new.

He started to laugh without knowing why.

Maybe it was the realization that he shouldn't be dwelling on something so small, but he suspected it was something more sinister. Maybe he had finally started to go mad. He fell asleep with a smile on his face.

When he woke up, six hours later, his thoughts were taking their time catching up with him. Everything felt automatic. Even with the bustle of those making their way to the leisure district early, there was a sense that the rest of the world was one step removed. Reality itself felt a little blurred, and consequently became a lot easier to deal with. He was well on his way before he really knew where he was going. The scene of the murder that had never occurred was only a few stops away.

The northern sectors were still under development - vast, glimmering towers stood proudly next to centuries-old rubble that was cordoned off, marked for future construction. You could never be sure, but the consensus was that the north was designed with those who preferred a little less background noise in mind. The sounds of the city faded away here - there was the faint roar of the freeway and an intermittent chorus of crickets, but little else. If you wanted to bludgeon someone to death at their front door, you'd have to find some way to keep them quiet.

The victim had only been three floors up, so Tim took the stairs. There was the smell of some unfamiliar spicy food wafting from one of the ventilation ducts, and the sound of his own heartbeat as he neared the right corridor. Every muscle in his body tingled. He was a cat waiting for the right moment to pounce.

As soon as he turned into the corridor, he saw it. A hulking, black security barrier, stretching from the ceiling to the floor, covering the entrance to the victim's apartment. Without thinking, his investigative instincts kicked in. His clenched fist was knocking on the door of the next house along before he could make up his mind.

A woman answered, the life drained from her exhausted frame and an instant disdain for Tim's uniform. Her hair was slicked back. She held a baby in one arm and waved off her two redheaded kids with the other, and after airing a handful of unrelated complaints, told him that there had been an infestation. No, she didn't know what - cockroaches, probably. You still got them around here, sometimes. Tim frowned, thanked her, and left.

He knew he was being lied to, but for some reason it didn't bother him. Even something like this - going out of his way to have his questions answered - was uncharacteristic behavior, given that his regular duties involved dealing with crimes he directly witnessed. Tim's one need, though, was that things run consistently, and that was why the previous night had thrown him off. Something - for whatever reason - had fallen through the cracks, and that small fact had burrowed into his unconscious like a maggot. There *were* no cracks. It felt toxic.

He needed a day off to reset his routine. A quick call to the office, and he was speeding back home, staring listlessly at the buildings rushing by, at a hundred thousand worker ants going out to play, all of them unaware that they could be stamped on at a moment's notice.

His thumb slid over the pad to his apartment and the door unlocked, each light fading on as he moved into the house. He didn't even have a moment to think when he saw her. She just started talking.

"Sit down, Tim."

She was his age - maybe a little younger. She wore an oversized, red hooded jumper and blue jeans. An androgynous face was made more so by her close-cropped auburn hair, and she looked bored - impatient, even. He wasn't sure what to do.

"Don't worry, this'll be brief." She began wandering the apartment, picking over it absent-mindedly. Silence filled the room. After three, maybe four minutes, Tim broke.

"Excuse me, I-"

She looked up, confused. Then, understanding slowly dissolved into her expression.

"Oh. Mm. Of course," she smirked, idly inspecting her fingernails before staring unflinchingly at him, "I forgot about the whole introductions thing. Erica Hazel. I work for the Central Bulletin?" She was looking at him as if that was all she needed to say as justification for breaking into his home. "Fuck, you try and get a little recognition and - so, you don't read the news. That's fine. You're still not sitting down."

Tim sat. For a moment, Erica's eyes were glazed as she checked her specs, and her relaxed expression turned to one of concern. He could hear the metro sliding past outside. He wanted this woman gone - his eyes were beginning to droop, and he could feel his anxiety coming on. Never mind the fact that someone had entered his home without permission

- it was being too exhausted to protest that set him on edge. "Is there a reason why you're here?"

She blinked and refocused, apparently surprised that he was still there. "Sorry, I... hm. Oh! Yes. The murders."

A sense of validation crept through his veins like ice. Murders, plural.

"Yes, I know, how could I possibly know about the second, *was* there even a second, isn't your mind playing tricks on you, et cetera, et cetera - feel free to get it all out if you have to. No? Nothing?" Tim was looking at her intently, a cacophony of raw emotion resolving itself into a single black glare. "Right. Then let's go with murders, because I know that it was leaked to you and - ha - me. But it's you I'm more curious about. I'm not sure I'm really the story here. At least, I hope not. Think of me more as, um... what's his name? Hermes?"

"Why does no-one else know about it?" She glared at him.

"Boring question, Tim. Most people don't know a lot. Look, I've got to go, but I got a message from an anonymous source earlier today that all but confirms the location and time of the next murder." He felt a sliver of GPS data drop into his inbox. "The current projection says it'll happen around seven, so I'd get there about seven-thirty. Any earlier and you really don't want to be there, unless you're planning to stop it. Though if it was me, I wouldn't do that. You'll get questions about why you were there to begin with, and if you out me as your source then I've already got an alibi ready that says we've never met. Also," she said, looking at her feet, "I dunno. There's something about all of this. I feel like maybe now might not be the best time to act unpredictably. Oh - and try not to get there much later than eight. Don't want to miss the party."

She began walking towards the front door. Tim felt glued to his chair. She stopped, just before rounding the corner, and faced him, as if seeing him properly for the first time.

"I'm sorry. Busy night. I'd explain everything in detail, but I'm... not sure I should."

"What?"

"I - this must all be a bit... weird. Maybe you shouldn't go after all, I just - it's hard to gauge this stuff, y'know?" Tim didn't know, and it showed on his face. "I really have to go. You have the address. I'll, um, let myself out." She teetered awkwardly, turned on her heel, and sped out the door.

Tim exhaled, and shakily got to his feet. The address was sitting there in his head, burned into his memory as soon as he saw it. Just another apartment building, but one with the potential for horror. His brain was a jumbled mess, and the only thing he could think of to numb it all was sleep. He staggered to his room, climbed into bed fully dressed, and made the one decision he was able to make - a refusal to deal with the world until he next woke.

Hours of restless sleep passed, and the world was still there when he awoke. He felt sluggish, forgetting to wake his specs, consequently not discovering the flashing critical error messages, the mass of impenetrable code, or the mad dash of dead pixels that had no hope of ever making sense. It was still light outside, but the noise was beginning to pick up.

Nothing shook the feeling. It was as if he was drugged - while showering, he felt as if every drop of water was waiting for his recognition before splashing against his body, and no matter how hard he scrubbed he couldn't feel clean. He brought his hands up to his face, and behind the stubble his pores were open, gasping for some relief against the humid, sticky air. His own skin felt like an ill-fitting suit. Without thinking, he dressed, and walked out. The only thing he could think about was the address.

Work was far from his mind. He hadn't even called in sick, and no doubt within the hour he would be getting frantic calls asking where he was, all of them silenced until he logged back in. Tim's anxiety was far away from those concerns. He felt paranoid on the metro. People seemed to be edging away from him. He hadn't looked in a mirror in days - was he really that intimidating? He spotted stubble and hooded eyelids in the faint reflection in the window, and remained silent as the train sped across the city.

Before the week had started, most of the apartment buildings around the city had just felt like hollow structures. People presumably lived in them, but Tim's social life was kept within the confines of his job - there were no late-night house parties, no furtive one-night-stands, just a simple routine. In one week, he had seen enough dank, dimly-lit corridors to last a lifetime.

As he began walking into the latest, he could hear his own heartbeat. There were distant voices. Without waking his specs - flashing more desperately than ever - he knew it was seven exactly. The voices became clearer. They sounded unhurried, calm, professional. A door was open, a few meters further away. The meters became kilometers. Space was dilating around him. It snapped back when he reached the door, and saw the corpse. He was too late.

Everything immediately felt out of sync.

The body was gruesome and contorted, a single blow to the back of the head caving in the skull. He had once been a tall, clean-cut man, stubble on his blood-flecked cheeks and broad shoulders. There was no question that he had been taken by surprise; someone of this man's stature could have easily fought off most people. There were stirrings of the horror of the first victim, but it felt somehow overridden by the sounds coming from further in, those same methodical voices talking over the sound of terrified, inhuman whimpering. Morbid curiosity overpowered nausea for the first time.

Tim silently stepped over the body. There was a deep undercurrent of quiet terror lurking somewhere in the back of his mind.

They were in the next room. The door was closed. Tim pressed his ear to it, and the voice sounded oddly familiar. That whimpering in the background appeared to be going ignored.

"... the fuck did this happen?"

"Jesus, I've told you - this wasn't our fault, we're just here to clean up. You know this wasn't planned."

"Doesn't seem fair. Still - I suppose it's a minor hiccup."

"There's a corpse at the front door that I think would beg to differ."

"Again - I think you're missing the bigger picture. We've contained the fatalities, and managed to shoehorn in a meaningful end for one of ours, and if I'm right, then we should be getting his entry just about...."

Tim stood in the doorway, having flung it open, his mouth open, eyes wide, trying to assess the situation before him.

"Now. Hello, Tim."

He knew the man and woman standing in front of him. Both clad in suits, the man looked disheveled, scratching the back of his head and avoiding eye contact. The woman looked grim, but cool, her hair tied up, revealing sharp cheekbones and a penetrating gaze. She turned to face Tim, allowing him a moment. On the floor behind her, drooling, softly whining, his limbs splayed and his expression vacant, was -

"Simms?"

There was still blood on his hands. He didn't look up at the sound of his name.

"He can't hear you, Tim. We just needed you to recognize him before -" she jerked her head, the man's expression glazed over, and Simms disappeared into a million tiny particles, a heap of burnt ash on the floor. There was no sound. Tim stumbled backwards, but didn't run. He couldn't. His mind was screaming at him to get out, but his arms and legs had turned to jelly. He fell against the wall, and slid down to his knees.

"Cuffs?" It was the man. He couldn't place him, but he felt uncomfortable just looking at him. It was clear that the feeling was mutual.

The woman smiled, the expression looking alien on her face, forced.

"I don't think we need them, do we?" She crouched, almost eye level. "I don't think you're planning on running."

Words finally escaped Tim's mouth before he could think them through.

"Who are you?"

"Try not to laugh when you hear me say this, but really: who we are is not important. What's important is who you are when you walk out of this room."

Confusion set in, followed by fear. "I won't say anything, I-" the woman laughed.

"I know you won't, and even if you did it wouldn't be a problem. No - what I mean is that as it stands, you have an opportunity. Mostly one of convenience, I won't lie, but an opportunity nevertheless. We need someone to fill the role of - well." She nodded to the mound of human remains on the floor.

"Do I have a choice?"

"You always have a choice, Tim. You should consider this as sound advice. We can ensure that you have a long, fulfilling life, and that you never go through anything like this again if you take it. You know how this all works." She sounded confident. The man nodded along next to her, the faintest hint of hesitancy behind his eyes. It went unnoticed.

He couldn't place them, but he knew that the two people in front of him were from much higher up the food chain, privy to information he could never hope to access. He could ignore them and leave, but he knew it would be the stupid thing to do. The terror of the situation - the body outside, the remains of his employer a couple of meters away from his feet - gave way to the feeling that he was innocent again, in the presence of people he could never hope to possibly understand, but who guaranteed his safety. His head down to hide his tears, his whole body beginning to shake, he nodded wordlessly.

*

You enter your new office to the sound of applause. A desk with your name on it sits in the middle of the room, and the sun streams in through the floor-to-ceiling windows. There is no trace of the previous occupant - no suggestion that there ever *was* one. Weeks of paranoia begin to settle, and a sense of comfort creeps in - the sense that you're in the right place, that you were always meant to end up here. You sit down, and slide open your agenda for the day.

You get married. A few dozen turn up to your wedding - enough for it to feel like a party, but not quite large enough to be intimidating. There are no children in your life, but it's a choice you're both happy with - a simple, stress-free partnership with the woman you love is enough. You move into a bigger apartment in a brighter part of town. On the weekends, you still go on walks around the leisure district at night.

Sometimes, you have nightmares. Everything is black, but there's the sense that your whole life is a jigsaw crudely forced together, full of pieces that have been broken up to fit. The feeling always passes within a couple of minutes of waking up. You forget how you got your job, your partner, your lifestyle - it just seems to fit. Your mind never stops to consider the suffering endured to keep things ticking along. You die happy, oblivious, a satisfied grin on your face.

DINING OUT

Part One

RAFI

I am uncomfortable in my own skin on Mondays. Mondays is for checking our stock and gearing up for the week, so I arrive an hour earlier and I've never quite shaken the sleep off. Two thousand vacuum-packed burgers. Ten boxes of fries, already pre-soaked in oil, waiting for a second coating once they're defrosted. Violet's Rest Stop is a place for comfort food, not class, and our customers know it. It's mornings like this, when the dew clings to everything and everyone is shaking off the weekend, when the most people seek us out for a bite before work.

Mark always arrives first, rippling muscles straining against a t-shirt that he still wears in the middle of winter. His brain only fires off enough neurons to keep him alive and functional, but he's good at heavy lifting and putting everything in its proper place. Tanks of syrup for the soda fountain. Industrial cooking oil for the fryers. Before the smell fills the restaurant, it's more like preparing a lab. There are some places that are just eerie when they're deserted. Schools, hospitals, amusement parks. Diners.

The neon strips underneath the counter flicker into life, yesterday's specials are scrawled out and replaced, and the tables are wiped down. The staff arrive, bleary-eyed, still waking up. There are the Grayberg twins, a couple of boys who I always delegate to kitchen work, a job they approach with enthusiasm that borders on irritating; Vivienne, Michael and Jonah, three equally drab-looking servers, able to blend in easily and not clash with the customer experience, and Sarah Sanderson. Oh, Sarah.

Sarah the sous-chef. At her interview, we'd laughed about the sibilance of her name and the job together, but after hiring her our relationship was simply functional in nature. At our busiest hours, there's barely time to take a breath, let alone have a conversation, and she's always gone by the time Mark and I close up. The memory of her laugh still lingers, though - every word she says to me has an electric undercurrent. Each glance provides a tantalizing hint of opportunity. Today is a public holiday, commemorating the creation of CAIN, and as she sweeps through the door there feels like some unspoken promise. Some silent communication as she smiles. *I want to celebrate.* Or *I want you.* Or at least *I woke up in a good mood.* At 7am, the festivities in the heart of the city are already coursing through the streets, but here on the edge of town there's an energy of a different sort.

SARAH
I wake up in a *mood.*

26

Jen packed up and left a couple of months ago without a word, nights after she discovered a couple of earlier indiscretions. Disappeared off the map. Didn't want to be found, I guess. Since then, I've been drifting. Over the last couple of years I've blundered through a few relationships, and after each one ends the first thing I always miss is the sex. Not even how the person in question fucked, but just the gerund, free from the messy tangle of emotions that flares up when you bring another brain into the mix: just *fucking*. That's what I get pangs for the day after they leave, and it takes a big distraction for it to go away. A dramatic accident. Some sort of inspiring vision quest. Or just fucking someone new.

Shit. This makes me seem kind of callous. Like I said. A couple of months. The background depression's set in as well by this point. I've been through too many breakups to make the same mental mistakes - I don't shift all the blame (only the amount I deserve), I don't try and rationalize a situation where everything would have worked out, and I don't get blindingly drunk and call them at four in the morning. Not often, anyway. It's cleaner these days. But still - losing someone sucks, even if you weren't meant for each other. You can get lonely, living by yourself when you're used to another body in the house.

When I wake up, I'm not lonely. I'm *hungry*. Again, this probably doesn't cast me in a great light, but just about anyone would do. It's CAIN's anniversary, and people are already going wild in the streets below. Already making eyes at each other from across crowded bars. I'm not one of them. I don't have that luxury. Every step from waking up brings me farther and farther outside the city.

On my way to work, I'm running through my coworkers,

calculating preferences and probabilities. Mark's off the list by default - I barely see him, and he's usually hulking around the cellar. Vivienne's pretty, but there's a rumor that she's a cultist, and no-one really knows their position on screwing around. The Graybergs are both eighteen, so they're out - teenagers are more trouble than they're worth. Also, twins freak me out. Michael's too uptight, and Jonah is another uncomfortable and embarrassing experience that I'd like to keep buried.

This leaves Rafi. My boss. Rafi, with his premature bald patch, and tired eyes, and quiet demeanor. I could do worse. And I'm not going another day without *something*.

RAFI

She slides her pants back on. Checks her hair. Meets my eye, sees me sitting there in my chair, wilting in post-coital awe, and laughs - not cruelly, but in reaction to the absurdity of the last twenty minutes.

I knew the moment she entered my office. The entire morning was punctuated by lingering glances, smiles held a little longer than necessary, and the occasional raised eyebrow - a dozen silent hints that spoke volumes. Although she kissed me first, there was no moment of shock, no pause to register what was going on. Everything felt inevitable the moment my door opened.

She was soft yet insistent, giggling and moaning against my chest. I can still feel where her nails dug into my back. We had started on the desk but moved to the sofa - a sofa that hadn't been used for months, and a plume of dust appeared as we fell, gasping and writhing.

She leaves, heading back to the kitchen, and I dress myself. My head is spinning. Alone in the office, I have no way to assess the context. That delicate build-up was established in silence, so this could be anything from a casual release to a sudden expression of interest. I spend the rest of the day trying to work on our annual budget, but I can't get the thought of her soft, pale skin out of my mind. The way it gave a little under my hands. How she shuddered against me.

As Mark and I close up for the night, I receive a message from her. Mark asks what I'm smiling at. I clap him on the back, barely containing my glee, and head home without a word of explanation.

SARAH

He was... *good*.

This is not my first job, and he isn't the first senior-level staff member I've fooled around with. There's a certain technique you attribute to managerial types after a while - grunting, oblivious to anything other than their own bodies, clean around the edges but lacking personal hygiene the more intimate you get. Rafi defied these. He was passionate. Overwhelmed, even. He *wanted* me, which sounds so self-deprecating when I put it like that, but it's still a shock. We were two imperfect bodies, together totaling something more than the sum of our parts.

I get home and kick off my shoes. The lights flicker on; the bulb on the porch still needs fixing. I'm wiped out, and not because I fucked my way through my lunch break with no time to eat; there are a few thoughts in my head that I haven't yet worked through. We didn't say a word, and that could be dangerous - he might think there was something more to it all, and there definitely (definitely?) isn't.

But.

There's something odd about this. Maybe it was just his style (light kisses on my neck, running his fingertips down my back, looking straight into my eyes as he slid inside me, what am I *thinking*) but my expectations were all thrown out of sync. It's like I'm irritated at him for not being terrible. It's easy to give up something unfulfilling.

My apartment feels empty tonight. I had an analog clock fitted when I moved in - revivalist, like my job - and it's the only sound when I settle into bed, *tick-tick-tick* as my eyes are wide open in the dark. At three in the morning, I pour a glass of whiskey and drink it too quickly. It burns in my throat and makes me cough, but the room warms a little, and I can finally sleep.

RAFI

Everything starts to feel sharper. We open the next day and I stand there by the neon *OPEN* sign for a full five minutes, feeling the glow through my eyelids. I have one more reason to get out of bed at the crack of dawn, and it's as if the whole day is charged with a new importance.

What continues as furtive fumbling in my office soon evolves into an affair - one neither of us can really explain, so we don't. We spend nights in each other's bed, driven by lust, hungry for contact. I wake up again and again thinking about her curves, the determined look in her eye as she looks down at my body, the afterimage of her gripping my shoulders and collapsing against me.

Eventually, we start to talk. Moans and sighs only get us so far. It's only after the seventh or eighth night at my house, my arm around her, both of us post-coital and laughing deliriously in the darkness, when we really begin to get to know each other. We emerged from different stations, seven years apart, but there's a strange emotional intimacy to those nights together.

There are arguments, occasionally - when I learn about her ambitions outside the service industry, and how the diner is a stopgap until her big break, jealousy of future unknown employers flares up and I can't quite contain it. Sometimes she has to rush off to other engagements - parties with people her age, constant visits to her forever-ailing grandmother - and while I keep quiet and still as she gathers up her things, passive aggression burning behind my eyes, it isn't long before muttering resentment creeps out of my mouth the moment after she leaves. Sometimes, the two steps it'd take to embrace her feel like a gulf.

But I feel *alive*. This new emotional maelstrom inside my head lights up every other aspect of my life. When I hand out bonuses at the end of the month, I feel the gratitude of my employees deep in my chest - even from Mark, who grins dumbly at his pay packet. Prior to all of this, I was content, happily passing the time, but now everything comes bundled with a frenetic, excited sense of urgency. There's a word I want to use to describe it, but it feels like a taboo to utter it: the last bastion before things really get serious. But it's there, hovering at the back of my mind. Taunting me, but leaving a grin on my face.

SARAH

Things turn sour fast.

My own fault. I set out with a specific goal in mind - one fun afternoon - and allow it to be twisted out of proportion because he has a nice smile and half-decent technique. And... *sure*, there are moments where it feels like maybe this isn't all that bad, but only until I see the next jealous flash in his eyes when I need to pry myself away from him. I begin to feel like I'm being kept in a cage. It's fucking claustrophobic.

There's no formal break - cowardice on my part, I suppose, but in the end it just hits both of us harder. I have to take the wounded-animal look a handful of times when my excuses become more and more pointed, and it soon gives way to quiet resignation when he gets the message. We still work together, but by the time I start my shifts he's always retreated to his office, only ever coming out to stick up the new schedule, always avoiding my eye when he does. I feel guilty at first, and want to apologize, but it soon gives way to resentment I can never articulate. He never treats me unfairly, and he never oversteps any boundaries. But for months, the silence is deafening.

Eventually, life goes on. I step outside at the start of May, and there's a shift in the air; the seasonal change, warmth on my face, and a steady increase in business relaxes my shoulders a little. The same week, I walk in and he's sat in one of the booths, reading the newspaper, and waves wordlessly as I walk in. There's even the trace of a smile, albeit a sad one. My apartment, once feeling empty, now feels bathed in sunlight and as homely as I expect it to be.

No rekindled friendship. Nothing so optimistic. But we coexist peacefully. The anxiety fades. And for the first time, I don't feel the need to fill the gap with another person.

Progress.

Part Two

DESPERATE

Some kind of self-preservation instinct kicks in - the need to preserve a working environment at a bare minimum. In some dark, locked room of my head there's part of me that's gnashing its teeth, screaming and shaking, but the only fear I can feel is that it might find a way to get out. As she gets colder and more distant, I just try and find more ways to distract myself.

It's easy at first, when the clues are subtle - I go for walks when she cancels on me, sink myself into work, keep myself ticking over. Then three weeks pass, and I realize that we haven't touched each other. That's how I find myself outside this den of iniquity. We came here once, a group of insatiable post-adolescent men in culinary training, still new to the city and everything it could offer. The sign above the door, hidden in a recess on a back street, was lit proudly back then; now, it flickers pitifully.

I step inside, and a deep bass thrumming immediately fills my ears, disorienting me. Instant drunkenness off sound, squinting through the red light at the woman sat behind the desk. She looks up at me dispassionately, and slides a screen open on the desk. You still see these every now and then - some neural transfers are more heavily regulated than others, and anything to do with sex has to pass through so many filters if you're using your specs. Touchscreens feel ancient, but at least they're discreet.

It's a survey. Preferences - gender, anthropomorphic degrees, illustrated with sliders and explanations. There was a rumor that when they first started manufacturing bots with tentacles, there was a three-month waiting list.

The list of kinks has doubled since my last visit, nine years ago. All of this used to be so rudimentary. We had stepped in as young men, baffled by the prospect of being able to express an interest in something that was programmed with different preferences or body types, and to have those desires fulfilled within ten minutes. Now, the level of choice is intimidating. All of the old ones are there: erotic massage, droid-on-top, a quaint volume slider that specifies how vocal you want your partner to be. But further down, things I only recall from late nights of boredom and drunken bar-room conversation. Flogging. Medical role play. Verbal degradation. Something called sounding - a word that I suspect has nothing to do with noise levels.

At the end, there are a few new options. A liability waiver, apparently conditional on selecting certain options, is greyed out, but lights up when I accidentally select *Wax Play* from the list. I panic and tap it again, and the box reassuringly fades from view again. A box is already checked, indicating that if it remains ticked then I consent to having my information shared across social networks and third party organizations. I smirk, shake my head, and remove the option, wondering how many people have flicked past it.

It takes a while to complete the form, and by the end of the night I go home feeling physically satisfied, but emotionally crushed. It doesn't matter how physically perfect bots are designed to look, how realistic their moans and grunts are, how hot, or tight, or wet it all feels - somewhere, I still retain the knowledge that there's something missing. But it beats furiously masturbating at home. It's something.

I still can't get her out of my thoughts.

Resentment, and ultimately resignation, only goes so far. The clock keeps ticking, and the sense of loss slowly fades, but nothing kills the more base desires; I can't stop the sudden flashes of memory when I see the curve of her hips, the way that her eyes smile even as her expression remains neutral. She removes her coat at the start of the day, and I remember the first night together, standing behind her, unbuttoning her blouse and slipping my hand inside her bra; she puts her hair up, and I remember grabbing it, grinning as she bucked her hips up against me, moaning; she barks orders at the rest of the staff, and I remember that same tone as she pushed me onto the bed, straddling me. Work becomes torment. I can't keep the thoughts of her from taunting me, so I retreat into my office, burying my head in paperwork, hoping that it acts as a shield between me and whatever carnal nightmare my unconscious wants to serve up. It doesn't. Nothing does.

PERVERSION

On Monday, I see a singular hair fall from Sarah's head onto the hard grey floor and time stops for a moment. When I stop and pocket it, only a few flickering connections are sparking; if I was asked why, I would look momentarily confused and stare at the follicle in my hand as if I'd picked up some foreign object. Maybe put it down to hygiene regulations, or rationalize another vaguely-plausible excuse.

No-one asks, though. I walk back to my office in a daze. It's only when I find myself halfway to the brothel that I realize what I'm doing. In my pocket, delicately curled around my finger, isn't just a hair - it's a promise of something darkly perverse. Even when I walk up to the desk, sweat on my brow, the words leave my mouth before I think of what to say.

"I want something special."

The same receptionist, her mouth a thin red line, raises her eyebrow.

"I want a particular cosmetic skin." When she reaches for the catalogue, I shake my head. "No - a custom one. Can you do that?" She breathes in, and the room appears to get colder.

"We'll need a DNA sample -" I excitedly begin to lift my hand out of my pocket - "and a copy of consent form B-928A. You can print them in the corner." I blink. She looks at me as if I'm an adult male learning to walk. "Biometric approval from the DNA subject. *Obviously*."

The color begins to drain from my vision, and I'm mentally scrabbling, desperately improvising my next move. I lean in, and look around nervously. "Are you sure there's no way to bypass that?" Poking out from under my wrist, leaning on the counter, is my cash card, openly displaying the live total of my personal funds. It's just a nudge, but she picks up on it and her cold look warms a little, the harsh line of her mouth turning upwards a little. Almost imperceptibly, she nods her head over to a door on the left, the chrome plate engraved with the words *"Engineers Only"*. She gets up, and follows me inside.

It's dark, even when the light - a single bulb hanging from the ceiling - is switched on. A terminal sits at the back of the room (more of a closet, really) monitoring the activities in every booth. It's a quiet night - only one or two seem to be occupied. The smell of stale, synthesized mucus makes me gag. She speaks, and my attention snaps back to her as I try and block out the chemicals filling my nostrils.

"This won't be cheap, you know. There are a lot of benefits to going the official route. There are subsidies for this sort of thing when it's above board." I smirk. Of course there are. "But... if you really can't obtain the authorization, I have a... friend. He might be able to fix you up."

"Who?"

"Don't know his name. You need to understand - you don't fuck with this guy. Once you decide you're in, there's no backing out." I nod. She stares into the middle distance, her eyes blank, and an address pops up in my inbox. "There. His office, if you can call it that. It's up to you what you do with it."

There's an awkward silence.

"Do you want any... I don't know, payment?" She focuses back on me, and I notice for the first time the slightly uncanny eye movement. She cocks her head and looks condescendingly at me. It's terrifyingly realistic.

"You need to understand - this whole exchange is a deliberate programming oversight so that my operators remain in the clear. I can't accept money for giving this information, but the man I've directed you towards can. He knows -" she looks me up and down, making me feel suddenly, oddly naked - "which of his clients are regulars, and which are referrals." She pauses. "I think we're done. Yes." She turns on her heel, and leaves the room, and I reluctantly follow.

In the waiting room, I glance through my specs. No messages from Sarah - not that I expected any. The address is there, unmarked. I notice that he lives about three kilometres in the wrong direction from the diner. Even at this point, bathed in an unnatural pink glow and deafened by pounding techno, I hesitate before downloading it. There's a sense of finality to this - that once I take this information, I'll be set on a course with no certain end. An unlicensed Virtual Interface with an illegal cosmetic skin is a felony if discovered, punishable by anything from a year underground to exile, depending on the offender. Hardly any are discovered - by their nature, they tend to be held privately - but nevertheless, I'm scared. The thrill of the risk involved hangs over me as I slot the address into my local contacts.

The muggy summer evening hits me as I leave, and it increasingly feels like I'm dreaming; as I step into the more dangerous side of town, everything becomes pure perception without analysis. Faces peer out at me, broad-shouldered men grinning eerily out from emerald hoods, weather-beaten women licking their lips ravenously, burned-out junkies shivering in the dirt, but I don't stop to think about my own safety. The only thing on my mind is getting to my destination.

Up three flights of stairs in a grime-filled tower block, I find it. I can hear babies crying, a series of musical thuds and squelches, a nihilistic cackle from the upper floors. It all fades to silence when I knock on the door, but I can't tell if the sudden absence is real or in my head.

The door opens a crack. Behind it is a hulk of a man, wearing a three-piece suit and a glowering look. He's customized his specs - the wire is a holographic streak of fire on the side of his head, and the capillaries in his eyeball pulse to an unknown beat.

"Yeah?" He doesn't seem happy to see me.

"I've been told you make, ah, custom goods here." He eyes me up, smirks, nods, and opens the door fully. It's dark inside; there's a maelstrom of LEDs at irregular points on the walls, lighting the way. "He's in the back."

Scrawled in UV paint on the door is the slogan "Abandon Inhibition All Ye Who Enter". Cute.

Inside is a lurid mess of gold and pink, the walls

plastered with pornographic screens, jewelry casually scattered around. In the center is a throne, scarlet upholstery and golden excess. The man sat in it (and it really is a throne, each leg carved with obnoxious flourishes, rare gems embedded in the back of the seat, a testament to having too much disposable income) has close-cropped hair, the same custom design on his specs, and blinks furiously as he devours reams of neural information. I open my mouth to speak, but he raises a finger, and gestures to the sofa running along the back of the room. I sit. Minutes pass. Finally, the display fades, he sniffs, blinks furiously to refocus, and turns to look at me, smiling.

"So... what *do* we have here? You'll be one of Ricki's, I bet." The name means nothing to me, but I assume Ricki is the proprietor of the brothel. "What is it, then? Are her kinks not hard enough for you? Need something that crosses the line? I've got a discount on castration if that's what, ah, gets you going." I flinch at the word. "OK, so perhaps not. What do you want, then? You haven't said a thing."

"I want to obtain a cosmetic skin of someone without their knowledge. Can you do that?"

He looks deadly serious for a moment. I suddenly realize that the man from the doorway is blocking the entrance, his arms folded, shuffling from one foot to the other. Behind those red eyes, I can see the cogs turning. Then, he starts laughing - slowly, at first, but breaking into a roar.

"Oh, boy... that is *delicious*. Goodness me. I've had some bizarre requests, but... that's really quite something. She doesn't know? Who is - ah, never mind. Not my business. I assume you have some DNA?"

The hair is still wrapped around my finger. I gesture my hand towards him, and he delicately picks it off, frowning.

"This get pulled out or did it just fall off?"

"It fell out. I couldn't exactly pull her hair." He raises an eyebrow. "We aren't together. Anymore."

He shakes his head. "It's difficult to extract DNA from hair unless there are residue cells from the rest of the body. I'll have to check. Give me a minute." He jumps up, and disappears through a door so low he has to crouch to get through. I can hear moaning from the screens around me, but none of this feels remotely erotic, just the product of a pornographer's fever-dream. I'm beginning to slide back to reality, when he resurfaces, beaming and swaying a little. I can see the trace of some fluorescent liquid trickling down his chin.

"You lucky boy. There's nothing at the root, see, but there were a couple of skin cells clinging on, and -" he pinches the space around his eye and spreads his fingers in front of him, and there, hovering in the center of the room, is a flickering 360-degree model of Sarah, nude, her arms outstretched and her face blank. He senses my sharp intake of breath, and nods. "That's her then, I take it. I wasn't sure - she isn't exactly my type. It should be fairly easy to synthesize that, though. Now. Time to fill in the blanks." I narrow my eyes. "All I can mirror is her cosmetic features - everything else is a blank slate. We have to figure out what you're into. I always like this bit." His eyes gleam.

And like that, in a neon-streaked grotto on the bad side of town, I methodically run through the full gamut of my fantasies. By the time we're done, he looks disappointed.

"You know, we usually get a kinkier class of character around here. You're so... *pedestrian*. If it wasn't for the context, I'd wonder what you were doing here."

He spreads his arms wide, and snaps the rotating model

shut with a clap of his hands. He downloads my address, and the monster of a man - still staring at me, his eyes bulging rhythmically - escorts me out, his huge, meaty paw pressed against the small of my back. In my inbox is an unsigned confirmation. *Two days. No guarantees, no refunds.* Despite all this, and the feeling that I might have just been scammed, I feel light-headed and giddy, tempted to skip home past the leering tramps and the scornful jeers and squawks from a thousand different directions.

It takes so long to get to sleep. My heart thuds against my chest as I slip into unconsciousness.

REVELATION

I feel guilty when I see Sarah walk into the diner the next morning. Some impish demon rests on my shoulder, waggling its bony fingers and chuckling to itself, nagging dread accompanied by some unspecified thrill on the horizon. I don't think she notices when I avert my eyes - things have already been awkward between us. We keep things professional. The demon snickers to itself when I think that.

The next forty-eight hours crawl by. The first night, I lie in bed awake, watching the seconds tick by, wondering if I haven't done something terrible. But then I rationalize it all, and it feels better - here's a perfect solution, where no-one has to know and I get some meaningful release. When the delivery van pulls up outside my house at four in the morning, and two dead-faced men spend three hours installing the CPU and disinfectant chamber in the back room, a cacophony of unholy mechanical screaming and the tinny sound of chart-topping radio somehow eking its way through, all I feel is excited. They leave without saying a word, not even stopping to ask for a tip. The truck speeds off into the night, and in their wake is something new. Something fresh. I can already feel myself stirring.

On the side of the CPU, a long cuboid object that houses the bot - can I call it Sarah? - there is a progress bar, slowly inching along, one percent at a time. I know that what lies inside is nothing more than a realistically rendered textured mesh, a mass of secretions, complicated physical trickery and visual similitude, but that's not what it feels like. It feels like I have a guest.

At 9:57am, when my back is sore from sitting in the glow of the machine, and my excitement has reached critical mass, the lid opens.

WELCOME

She - it - no, *she* - stands there for a second, glassy-eyed and booting up. Then life, or something indistinguishable from it, sparks and she's looking at me.

"Hello."

I'm surprised that she speaks first, but not unhappy. Nervousness clings to me. I smile back, lacking a little confidence, and stumble out a "hi." She blinks, and narrows her eyebrows, then looks back to me. I'm finding it hard to breathe.

"So. I suppose I need a name. It's noted in my diagnostics that you've indicated a preference to call me *Sarah* - before I lock this in, do you want to change your mind?" I shake my head. "I'm afraid I'll need a verbal confirmation, darling." I jump, and she grins. I can feel myself stirring at her sudden intimacy. I'm not sure why, but I hadn't expected an emergent personality so soon. I whisper a "no".

We sit down. We talk about her technical capacity. I undress, and we move from position to position, from slow and gentle to hard and feral. Part of me knows that she's establishing a sort of methodological framework, assessing every shudder and moan for future reference, but in the moment it doesn't matter. It feels real.

Only when the morning light starts to seep in through the windows and she slips with a wink into the disinfecting chamber does a little of the magic go. But I'm so flooded with endorphins, lying on the floor with a stupid grin plastered across my face, that it hardly seems to matter. I'm satisfied beyond belief. I don't just have Sarah back - I have something *better*.

UNCANNY

It's not always simple.

On the third night, after my body feels completely spent, we lie there bathed in a post-orgasmic aura and I ask if she can spend the night in my bed. She looks at me, her eyes full of warmth, and explains that she can only remain autonomous if she's allowed to recharge, and that a full session only lasts twelve hours, and that I would have to manually intervene if she were to stay with me past 5am.

I rest my hand on her face, and kiss her. I tell her that it's fine, that I'll carry her if I need to. She closes her eyes for a moment, and when she opens them again she nods and moves closer to me. Even with her in the house, the loneliness sometimes creeps in, but as I feel her warm, beating heart against mine, her arms wrapped around me as she sleeps, I forget the truth - that there is no heart. Sleeping, for her, requires just as much processing power as the kind of stamina-defying rough sex that defined the previous hours.

My breath catches in my throat when I see her the next morning. She doesn't quite feel cold, but the glassy, neutral expression is back, her limbs relaxed, a corpse perfectly preserved between the sheets. I don't know why, but I start to cry - great, shuddering sobs as I wait for the disinfecting chamber to finish its cycle. It's hard to parse the reason why. There is some moral concern here, but it slips out of my grasp every time I try to put it into words. *This harms no-one.* The words feel like a mantra. There is, sometimes, the sense of creepiness, that a few miles away lives a woman who has no idea that her cosmetic twin is engaging in delicious acts of deviance with the man she left behind, but *she doesn't know*, and for some reason that keeps things vaguer. A little more neutral. She doesn't know. She can't know.

When I slide her into her pod to recharge, a flicker of life returns to her eyes. Everything is placed into a low-power state while she's being prepared, but as the lid closes I swear I can see the trace of a reassuring smile.

ROUTINE

When I look back on this later, I can't help but think that it took such a short time to sink into regular beats - for Sarah to become a regular part of my life again.

There is still some uneasiness at calling her Sarah. We experiment with S for a while, a slightly dehumanizing distinction, but there are enough reminders to keep the two distinct without obfuscating things further. I know that the Sarah at home is not the Sarah at work, and while it sometimes feels like the two merge in the throes of orgasm at home, I never misstep at work. At the back of my mind is the knowledge that Sarah the companion doesn't blink when I accidentally reference things about which she would have no knowledge, only nodding and smiling. I know that if the two met, she would carry on nodding and smiling while the Sarah I work with would be outraged. *A human reaction*, I can't help but think, but before long the thought doesn't make me feel guilty at all. Avoiding the messiness of humanity is what keeps me feeling balanced, sates my loneliness, and drains my libido.

The slide into normalcy is what convinces me that all of this is okay. The fear of discovery fades to black. We work out a subroutine where Sarah will automatically return to her basic diagnostics when she falls to 2% charge, and the feeling of her sliding gracefully out of bed half an hour before I open my eyes feels so much more human than waking up in her lifeless arms.

The one thing that continues to excite me is the purpose for which she was designed. Each night, my horizons are expanded. I begin to learn the tantalizing possibilities of pain, the full extremities of pleasure, and the bodily places one can go when a lithium ion battery replaces human stamina. Each night, as I get into my car, waving Mark off last, I can feel myself getting hard long before I get to my front door. Each night, she's there, waiting for me, ready to get to her knees and unzip my pants, or grab my neck and slam me against the wall, or lean in demurely to kiss me, the moment she analyses my responses. At one point, I think of going back to the stranger who arranged all of this so I can thank him, but I think better of it. He was paid handsomely enough.

Things feel safe again. Business experiences a sharp rise when CAIN releases the latest cohort above ground, and the appearance of so many new young faces adds a fresh energy to the air that appears to affect everyone. One day, I smile over at Sarah - a kind of resigned, we-made-it-through-unscathed smile, and she smiles back. There's no promise there, and we both know it. Just a smile. An acknowledgement that things are fine the way they are.

Mark leaves. He confesses one morning that he's won a spot as a dancer in the National Ballet following a midnight audition, and after we pick ourselves up from laughing hysterically we wish him well. It feels like such an absurd choice that it almost fits. Once he departs, no-one replaces him for a while, so I'm always alone at the start of each shift, but it feels okay. There's a sliver of *something* missing, still, but it doesn't really affect my happiness. Each evening, when the autumn light streams in through the windows and bathes the counter in the sunset glow, there's this perfect emotional alignment where I realize that I could live this life until my last breath and have no tangible sense of loss.

Part Three

Left at the lights.

Rafi turns out to be a momentary, fluid blip in an otherwise dry stretch that continues indefinitely. I worry for a while that my standards are too high, that maybe my physical age - twenty-nine, decidedly post-adolescent and only appealing to boys whose raging hormones far exceed their emotional maturity - is starting to act against me, that maybe I'm more irritating to others than I previously thought, but those thoughts usually fade. There's just a dearth of opportunity to connect with others; at the end of the night, I'm usually too tired to go out to bars, and the thought of going out and resuming the trend of casual hook-ups ending in train wreck relationships is nauseating. Rather than turn me off relationships, the almost-success with Rafi serves as the seed for a burgeoning desire to find one that works.

Past the Ritter Building, across the intersection.

It's hard to gauge when I start to question past decisions, but when I do, I'm cautious. I need to be careful when reflecting on relationships, as I tend to internalize the faults of others and think of them as poor reflections of my character. But something doesn't feel right about how things ended with Rafi. Maybe it's the respect and distance he gives me after we split - it doesn't feel like the usual template for jealous boyfriends. And there's the fact of the awkward situation I find myself in later with a so-called friend, who was suddenly and horribly open about the fact that he'd only bought me coffee in the hope that he could get my clothes off. As I back away, shaking my head, I can't help but remember Rafi, face red, trembling, telling me to stay away from people like that.

There is still enough to question his judgment. His active desire to constrain my hopes for the future, even if they were rooted in keeping me around. The awkward refusal to meet any of my friends, combined with the look in his eyes whenever I wanted to hang out with them. It never feels like I've made the *wrong* decision, but I begin to wonder if I've made the right one. The more comfortable work gets, the more that his cautious, post-breakup respect transforms back into the usual friendly work atmosphere, the harder it is to sleep at night.

Over the Viaduct.

As the last customers leave one night, he smiles, and

something clicks within me - that regardless of whether or not it's going to work, I know that anything we tried wasn't good enough. He was jealous, but I was distant - too wrapped up in my own thoughts to notice the man in front of me. We both deserve a second chance. Call it anger at myself for giving into selfish desires, founding a relationship on how his body felt rather than considering his mind, but it feels like we equalize a little - as we exchange that look, there's an acceptance that we're both flawed, and that if we'd only recognized this earlier then things might have worked out.

I get home, drop everything, change into some new clothes, turn on my heel and walk right back out of the door. And start driving.

Past a hundred identical condominiums, lit by the artificial glow of the city.

I tell myself that we're not going to fuck. It's less the fact of how things turn out that matters to me, and more what my intentions are going in. I want to sit down with him and talk. Have a drink. Actually get to know each other in an open and honest way, without every sentence laced with poison.

Outside his house, I switch the engine off and breathe. My heart is pounding against my chest. The last time I felt this nervous was when I first came to the surface. There's so much tangled up in this moment - fear, and excitement, and the slightest thrill between my legs. I can feel myself flush.

I knock on the door. There's no answer, but it swings open, and immediately I can hear soft moans from the back of the house. Something propels me forward, towards the source of the sound.

And I'm not sure what happens next.

I'm still not sure.

My next lucid memory is crying, my teeth grinding against each other, driving home at top speed, confused and angry and bitter and overwhelmingly upset. Every time I go to breathe, another flash hits me. The restraints. Pound the steering wheel, struggle to stay on the right side of the road. His eyes, closed, blissful until he heard the door creak. Turn the music up, push a little harder on the accelerator. Her face -

Her face.

I make it as far as carefully pulling the car onto the side of the road, and then collapse against the wheel, my entire body shaking, suffocating on my own sobs. My head is pounding, because behind the immediate despair there are a thousand angry questions. I can't bring myself to deal with any of them. This is all too much. My body is shattered glass.

Part Four

The illusion was gone in nanoseconds. Everything slid into its terrible place in one moment, and the revelation was so powerful that I could only lie there, naked, slack-jawed with terror in my eyes.

She resigned, of course. No-one could blame her. And I paid a visit to an industrial landfill on the edge of town, renting a van large enough to house everything. Like disposing of a corpse, but one step removed. The strangeness of an empty house took days to wear off, but once it did everything set in, as if it had been waiting and escalating in the shadows while I fucked my way out of self-engagement.

Solitude only really works as a comparative, I soon discovered. I had spent most of my life alone without paying it a second thought, but now every waking moment brought flashes of anxiety, waves of regret, slow burning anger - at her, at myself, at *something*.

Despite all that - despite the rage, and the bottomless despair, and the sudden castration of any future easy contentment - I don't think any of that led me here. Standing here, with the wind rushing in, around, out of my open mouth, turning my throat dry, I feel calm. Like this is a natural conclusion. As if my grinning skull is a fitting, haunting end to a life lived poorly. Basking in the knowledge that the joke, in the end, was on the rest of the world.

I tried to rationalize it all, but - but there was so much *shame*. Guilt and embarrassment are poor bedfellows when you try to engage in any therapeutic help. I would turn a corner, come to terms with my loss, and then remember that I was grieving the loss of something grotesque along with her flesh-and-blood original. Then guilt at feeling the absence of something so warped in the first place; then arrogance, throwing up tenuous moral arguments to justify the whole fucking mess; then confusion, sliding toward another night without sleep.

So I tried my best to forget. She was gone, and whispers from the kitchen suggested that her life had gained forward momentum. I could never fully erase the look on her face, an expression that sparked white-hot shame as soon as I thought about it, but I could let it fade. And it did. New details came along, and her fury, burning with color, became a watermark.

Jonah was promoted to sous-chef, and we took on a

couple of kids - eighteen-year-olds who somehow defied the long-held view that the diner was some kind of purgatory for artists with big dreams. Upon their arrival, their lifelong ambitions were realized, and they took to imposing their style on the place. It wasn't unwelcome, but it was also strange - a new attitude that didn't fit with the past. It took a few days to get past the initial unease, but after a while their zeal became infectious.

And yet.

It felt like an arc, you see. There was a tragic chord, a brass rumble of anxiety, and then a drone of normalcy as the color faded away. This felt like the dénouement before the end. A chance to collect my thoughts and act rationally - to see the end of the road with clear eyes before rumbling to a stop. I'd known that it was going to end here from that first creak of the door to my bedroom, but what was a chaotic and confused vision eventually settled into something more manageable. A sense of certainty. No fear in the face of death.

There's still something that makes me linger here, though, the one-hundred meter drop off the viaduct a step away, that screams at me to think twice. I'm not sure what it is. Not defiance. Yes, she had found a new life, but it was despite the scar tissue, not because of it. Moving on had been an active choice to escape my destructive force. My raging libido. My empty head. She was out of the way of any further harm, but that didn't discount the damage done.

Something else, then. A glimmer of something behind a wall of shame. The possibility of repentance - not through half-baked apologies, but through an active change in direction. I had learned about a dark world ready to cater to the desires of truly unpleasant people, and maybe I could take some shaky first steps toward dismantling it. Maybe.

Next to oblivion, a life of constant shame, hard work and no gratitude or self-pity is hardly an exciting alternative. The only thing it has going for it is that it might be the right thing to do.

I breathe in.

DEATH IN EXILE

I

"Dead?"

Two dark shapes huddle over me. Black spots against a blacker sky. Everything is a jumbled mess.

"Nah. Hanging on, I think. Ted isn't gonna be happy."

Scroll back. Further. Words creep out from shadows. Exile. Miscalculation. Integrity. Garforth. *Thirst.*

"C'mon, we can't just leave her here. Remember what I was saying about keeping standards? Ah, look at the lass. She hasn't seen a drop in days."

Sorry.

Sorry?

II

"Sorry, but this has put us in a - well - *very* awkward situation."

"Come on, we all know that the Strategy's designed for fuckups like this. And besides, it's *not my mistake*. You *told* me to kill him. Shouldn't it be you that's held responsible?"

A nervous smile. Two beads of sweat running symmetrical paths down his forehead.

"I think we both know that's not going to happen. And - yes - there is a contingency system in place for things like this, but even the best damage control scenario available to us involves..." (he shifts focus to his specs. I could strike now, and take my chances. Not sure it would get me anywhere, though - he looks strong, and even if I won, there would be others here in seconds. I never banked on hand-to-hand combat) "... seven more pre-conclusive deaths, the entire region's uncertainty quota reaching 13%, and national trust in CAIN declining by 0.3%. Better they pin the blame on you than society's operating system, don't you think?"

"Zero-point-three doesn't exactly sound high."

"Zero-point-one could be catastrophic."

The cuffs bite into my hands. Wait, no - maybe I remembered that wrong. Either way, something feels uncomfortable. Was I drugged? No. I was at home. I remember that much. Then-

Wait. Too many questions here. Rewind a little. Keep things simple.

III

"Ordinarily, we'd be feeding gas into your room and insinuating this into your unconscious memory, but I can already tell that's not going to wash with you."

This is more like it. I'm eleven. In front of me is the same man - less worn, handsome in a paternal way. He speaks in a low voice, seductive yet clear. His sheer physical charisma drowns out the other woman in the room, who opens and closes her fists, irritated.

"So let me give you an example, instead. A man goes through his life making a positive difference to the community. He experiences backlash from people with a vested interest in fear and unease, but he succeeds despite them. On the morning of his sixty-fifth birthday, he earns the crowning achievement of his life - a real mark on the world that he can call his own - and feels a sense of completion, as if he has come to as natural an ending as anyone could have hoped for. What then?"

"Who are you?"

"We'll get to that. First, think about this. If this man goes on to live another twenty years until his natural death, twenty years of inactivity thanks to failing health and inevitable decline turn him inwardly bitter. This man spent his life as an activist, and while he has a lifetime of achievement behind him, he *knows* that there's always more to be done. But he can't! He obsesses over the days where he would lead rallies, give inspiring speeches to the next generation, and begins to hate himself for the wreck he's become. He dies feeling ashamed of himself, open-ended with no resolution, forgetting his life's work, because of a couple of decades where he was rendered useless. Or...."

"Or what? And you never said what this guy did in the first place."

"That doesn't matter. It's a hypothetical with precedent, that's all you need to know. Here's the alternative: on the day after his sixty-fifth birthday, he's gunned down in his prime by an unknown assailant, someone who is widely assumed to be one of the few people adversely affected by the man's work, but who is never found and disappears without a trace. His death is at the hands of a shadow. The man dies not only as a hero, but as a martyr, and knows as the life leaves his body that this is as natural an ending as growing old and dying in his sleep."

There's a silence right about now. He looks very pleased with himself. He's a preacher delivering a sermon, oblivious that the congregation are profoundly disinterested in what he has to say.

"And?"

"We want you to be a shadow."

Another silence. This time with a side order of tension.

"You want me to kill people."

"For the right reasons, yes. We know you'd be good at it. We know you've already thought about it. Confess: that story I just told you, it already feels familiar, right?"

It does, but I don't say anything. History is a murky place, filled with inaccuracies and obfuscations. When it comes to the centuries before we retreated underground, we have to rely on the fuzzy data our ancestors kept, but names like Kennedy, King, and Gandhi still stand out in clear bold type. I know about people whose deaths were almost as significant as their lives, littered around a civilization that lived exclusively on the surface. But. The world these days is supposedly very different. We're supposed to accept that the past has little to teach us. It's supposed to be a cautionary tale.

"In answer to that question," the man says, reading me like an open book, "the city above you is still one with a vast variety of lives. Meaning takes shape in a limitless number of ways, and some of them require high-profile assassination."

I pause at this.

"What about me?"

"You get the security and anonymity you've always wanted. See this?" He brushes his arm, and vanishes from sight, replaced by a balding, middle-aged man with tobacco-stained teeth. It's grotesque, but utterly convincing. "Yours. This is not technology that officially exists. The Watch don't even know this exists." Even his voice and posture have changed, and I shiver a little at the possibilities. He scratches his nose, and reappears in his usual, svelte form.

The thought of the world above cripples me with terror when I think about engaging with other people. The thought of exposing myself to others - opening up, or sharing heartfelt conversations, or giving out my address to people who might use it - fills me with nausea. The thought of trying to connect plunges me into a dissociative state. The man sat in front of me knows that I put as much stock in the sanctity of human life as a mother of a small child puts in the weight of a fallen tree. Sometimes, others have to die for the greater good.

"That man I just described? We know that he's nothing like you. Some define their lives by building to one perfect moment, but we know that your ambition is a sense of peripheral constancy - a tightly-controlled life whose implementation feels effortless. We can give you that. You can live to ninety with a life like that. We won't even require your services that often - after all, too many newsworthy assassinations and people start to notice patterns." He laughs at this, then stops when he notices no-one joining in.

He sends an array of details - addresses, weapon details, maps - over to my inbox, where it sits. Static, cold information.

"One more thing. On our side, we call this your

induction. We usually rely on mild hypnosis and suggestion. In fact, you're the first person I've had to field questions from. But this isn't a job interview, and it's not an order. You are - and let me stress this - free to ignore every word I've said, and pursue your own life. But we'll be watching, either way. We'll try to align you with the greater good as much as we can, given your own agency. But, ah... think of this as a fast-track ticket."

I scan through the details. The first item in my inbox is the address of a silicone manufacturer. I don't question it.

"This should be the last time you see me. Think about it, okay?"

I leave seven years later, into the bustling hell of the world above, and give it four and a half seconds' thought before I start planning a route.

IV

Something is flickering. I'm in a tent. A woman - painfully skinny, without a single follicle on her head - sits next to my prone body, clad in a loose-fitting orange jumpsuit. There's a name badge pinned above her left breast. HELLO, MY NAME IS TEDDY. She clicks her tongue, and shakes her head.

"Fuck me, you look like you've seen better days."

My vision clears a little, making out the lantern in the corner, and outside, a few nervous glances peering out from the darkness. Teddy narrows her eyes, and gestures to a canteen filled with water resting beside my head. I pick it up - my fingers are trembling, weak - and press it to my lips. The unfamiliarity makes me cough. I can feel my hipbones straining against my skin with every movement. Every breath pushes against my ribs.

"It's okay. You're lucky. We're about to close our doors. You'll be surprised to hear this, but I was a community planner before I ended up here. Things like self-sufficiency, food rationing, delegation of responsibilities - they're all second nature. You put us at our limit. The next poor sod to lose her way'll have to fend for herself."

The disorientation hits me in waves. Her eyes are huge - cartoonish next to her slight features. So much is missing. I remember lots of walking. Panic. The loud *bang* of a towering gate slamming shut.

V

A loud *bang*, and mayoral candidate Tamsin Forrester drops to the ground, four hundred meters from my vantage point. I'm hidden in a construction site. Dust chokes the air, clinging to my clothes, camouflaging me. Through my scope, I can see aides rushing over to her as the crowd swells and collapses, as many dispersing as rushing to the scene out of morbid curiosity or the belief that a perfectly-angled bullet severing the brain stem might somehow be counteracted with a little hope and determination. I don't stay for the emotional fireworks.

My bank balance inflates reassuringly on the way home. My employer - a company who specialize in bespoke adult toys and aquarium sealants - has been particularly generous this time. Officially, I'm a quality assessor, and anyone examining my apartment would be suitably convinced. I spend, on average, about three hours in the office every year. I look entirely unassuming, even when I'm not cloaked, which is rare. I drop the weapon into a waste processing unit two blocks from the location, digitally scrubbed free of DNA evidence. Even as the bulletins roll in on the train, I can't help but smile - headlines like *Chaos in the City Centre* and *Police on Full Alert* reek of manufactured hysteria. No real threat. All the terrorists want right now is a stiff drink and a good night's sleep.

I chose an apartment purely on the basis of sound. The walls were cracked when I moved in, the sensors in dire need of recalibration, but stop for a second and all you can hear is the sound of your own breathing. Some would find it unsettling. I couldn't settle for anything less. A lot of comfort comes down to easily-changeable cosmetic differences, but there's only so much soundproofing you can do when cars race past twenty-four hours a day, or when drunks litter the hallways, or when your neighbors throw house parties to an alarmingly frequent schedule. All of those are absent here. I'm fairly sure that the neighboring apartments are vacant - that, or the people living inside are excessively, deliberately polite. Nothing since I moved in - no awkward, can-I-borrow-the-milk intrusions, no barely-concealed arguments... silence.

Some would call this lifestyle lonely. The thought never occurs to me. There's no seething hatred of civilization lurking under the surface of this skin, just lack of interest. I read books. For exercise, there are a thousand virtual walks accessible at the gym down the street, ready at the pulse of a transmitter, exploring places that were razed to the ground or ravaged by nature centuries ago. There are limits to what the city can offer me, but it's nothing that neural downloads can't solve.

VI

"So - what can you do?"

A haggard-looking man peers at me through watery eyes, blinking back dust. The bluntness of the question, along with the potential plethora of responses it invites, stuns me into silence for a moment. Eventually, I grimace and tell him.

"I kill."

He looks confused. "You hunt?"

"No. I - I used to assassinate people. Political figures, activists, high-ranking businesspeople. People whose lives needed to be wrapped up quickly." His expression shifts quickly from shock, to acceptance, to amusement.

"Not much call for that here, I'm afraid. Sounds like you were in the direct employ of CAIN - am I right?" I nod, almost imperceptibly. I notice my lip trembling, and stop when his eyes turn sympathetic. Days in, I'm still a starved wreck of a human being, but I won't crack. "Don't worry, we'll find something for you. I take it this means you're good with precision, huh?"

"Yes."

"'Yes.' Very to-the-point. I like you. Tell you what, we've got a small plant devoted to manufacturing microprocessors on the edge of the colony. Only a couple of others work there, and they aren't exactly noisy. It isn't rewarding work, but in a place like this everyone's got to make themselves useful. A lot of others started out in jobs a hell of a lot worse." He smiles, like he's on my side. I think that's his expression, anyway. He has so many wrinkles that his whole face has to shift with each emotion.

It's hard to judge people, especially in a place like this,

where such a dramatic reshuffling of priorities seems to be in place. SURVIVAL FIRST is stenciled in a scattershot fashion on walls, windows and banners, and there seems to be little infrastructure that deviates from that purpose. Everything feels freer, but that comes with a side order of intimidation. No safety net. The city shines only a few miles away, but it feels like an impossible philosophical divide.

VII

It's hard to figure out, with the benefit of hindsight, exactly what I thought when the order to assassinate Peter Garforth came through. He was a low-ranking public servant, perfectly ordinary, on an upward but otherwise unremarkable trajectory.

The order comes in at two in the morning. This, by itself, isn't cause for concern. They spell his name wrong - "Petr" - but a quick search identifies no other potential matches fitting the description. It's him. Still - something feels off. Or maybe I just remember it that way. It's all a little hazy.

His death is slow, but painless. I cloak myself as a waiter at a political fundraiser, and slip a slow-acting poison into his drink. By the time he leaves, he's reportedly complaining of a headache, but nothing more. He gets home, falls asleep, and doesn't wake up the next morning. The drama and intrigue comes from the press reaction - the poison is found in his system during autopsy, and it's lapped up as a whodunit crime caper, full of outlandish suspects and an increased rate of suspicion between friends. I don't know why his death is desirable. I don't know why the wider social effects were deemed appropriate. I don't care. I am a non-participant. I have no friends to keep an eye on, and it feels better that way. I trust that they know what they're doing, but even if they don't it's unlikely to have an effect on me.

Just another cog.

Peter Garforth. Such a straightforward name, but impossible to forget.

VIII

I am thirteen, now. Thirteen years of underground living.

```
ATTN:    ALL    INITIATES    IN    SECTOR
5/A51
CABIN DOORS WILL UNLOCK FOR ELEVEN
HOURS BEGINNING AT 7AM TOMORROW IN
THE INTEREST OF YOUR ENJOYMENT AND
SOCIAL    WELFARE.    CAIN    HAS    NOTED
THAT    CERTAIN    CITIZENS    OPT    FOR
SELF-INFLICTED    SOLITUDE    DURING
THESE    PERIODS,    AND    WOULD    LIKE    TO
REMIND    YOU    ALL    THAT    THESE    PERIODS
OF    RELAXED    SECURITY    ARE    FOR    YOUR
BENEFIT.
```

You can't predict how children will act. That's the knee-jerk reaction that washes over me every time something like this comes through the bulletins. It's the latest in a series of minor revelations that make no difference to my station, or my freedom, or - well - anything, really, but there's a grim comfort in knowing that you know a little more than the people who live around you. There are a couple of droplets of information I've deduced in my short time on the planet:

1. Rather than part of some grand mythos, CAIN is a massive artificial intelligence designed to reflect on genetics, social and emotional development, then guide the actions of others with a specific purpose

in mind. Not that this is really kept secret. It's more like there's a concerted PR campaign to shroud it in mystery and awe, so that people don't question its ultimate purpose. (Note to self: not quite sure what that is yet. Suspect it has something to do with Aristotelian philosophy, or the collected works of an old-world flickmaker called Michael Bay. Has something to do with the word "narrative", though, which I've seen on the occasional reflection from our supervisors' headsets.)

2. We're kept apart from the world upstairs until 18 because the onset of puberty makes us a little too unpredictable, and the aforementioned AI can't adjust quickly enough to our whims. The last time I exited my cabin, a boy called Tim was being openly hostile to my neighbor, Rafi, going so far as to pelt him with food; three weeks prior, the same Tim was caught by a supervisor in the local server room with his head between Rafi's thighs. Part of me wonders if people like Tim do a better job of navigating interpersonal relationships when they get to adulthood, but presumably the wider space allows for a little more personal contemplation. That contemplation might still be half-witted, but at least it's there.

3. I don't want - hm.

I don't want any part of this. I learned about superiority complexes three years ago, but I don't think this is that (even though I definitely do know more than everyone in this block, some supervisors excluded) - instead, it's more of a fear of engagement. I have put out feelers before, but even down here there are odd social customs that I can't quite engage in without feeling like I'm under a spotlight.

To begin with, I felt lonely. Over time, though, I began to see quite how much of that feeling came from outside constructs - those subtle digs to go out and "ENJOY YOURSELF" - and less from my own head. I keep fit. I read until the words swim in front of my eyes. I am thirteen years old, and this month I'll have watched my seven hundredth flick. There's a peculiar sense of achievement that I get from something like that, but successfully negotiating an encounter with another person just leaves me feeling hollow. I see their eyes glimmering with anticipation and warmth, and all I can think about is graphically deconstructing the pigmentation of their irises, finding the subtle shade between blue and black so I can change my cabin desktop when I return - finally - home.

At 7AM, three and a half seconds after I hear the automatic locks disengage, I switch the manual locks on.

IX

Assembling microprocessors is tedious, but things go at an easy enough pace. A few weeks in, I learn that organization among exiles is aggressively democratic, but somehow it seems to work. Everybody here is so *thankful*, I guess, and it makes sense - the vast majority left the city against their will, assuming that slow starvation was all that was waiting for them on the outside.

It's not just that, though. It's only noticeable because it's missing, but there's a particular tension that seems absent. Maybe it's that everything feels awkwardly bolted together - plenty of incompatible people sharing the same space, doing ill-fitting jobs and eating the same meals day after day - but with the disappearance of a perfect world comes a huge lift, as if perfection was a ridiculous goal to begin with. We are dust-streaked and tired, but content. Mediocrity is a standard anyone can comfortably reach.

I have nightmares, sometimes. There were corpses before I arrived. God knows how long they'd been chewed up by the environment. Most were skeletons. Some still had errant muscle fibers clinging on despite the futility of it all. Long nights in stakeout positions taught me the value of only consuming what you need, and my Exile Pack lasted what felt like weeks, but the temptation to munch through rations and let exhaustion overtake basic survival precautions was overwhelming. I still can't work out when I gave up, or how long I was lying there before the recon team saw me curled up, as if a fetal position might shield me from death.

This colony works, somehow. There is this odd space where I have to work out a compromise between functioning in a place like this and setting my wants aside, but for the most part it's manageable. Slowly, I learn to adjust to the noise. As each day passes, the sudden loss of a paternalistic guiding hand becomes more of a fondly-remembered way of life, belonging in nostalgia but not the day-to-day.

I still worry that my willingness to burn bridges comes from one isolated event. In a colony full of exiles, it follows that there's a deep mistrust of CAIN, even though we lived and breathed it until it chose to choke us out. The founder - Katia Prinsson - was a supermodel who developed alopecia and found her future crumbling before her eyes. With others, they were forced out for convenience's sake. William, the man who sits next to me on the production line and spends most of his days in silence, was an outlier - someone who had a change of heart, pursuing a career in banking rather than pornography and rising too far too fast. And I killed Peter Garforth. The wrong man, at the wrong time, and the only way to correct the balance was to refuse to cover it up.

X

Sixteen. Another social event. This time, they've made it so that access to food is restricted to the communal area, essentially forcing us out of our cabins. I still try and hold out as long as possible. Finally, when the noise fades and the hunger pangs are verging on unbearable, I creep out.

The lighting is harsher out here. Every blemish, organic or artificial, has a shadow. The smell of hot tomato sauce wafts down the corridor, and I can hear fumbling under blankets, enthusiastic conversation, muffled gasps behind sheet metal. Everyone seems to have left. Good.

In the communal area, there are a couple of steaming bowls of pasta left on the counter. A screen, muted, shows the evening news from the world above. It feels dangerous. I switch it off, and load my food onto a tray.

Someone clears their throat. I turn around, slowly.

Erica Hazel. This is the second time I've seen her. The first was by accident. Her hair is short. Spiked. Two pale brown eyes peer out, regarding me as if I'm some heretofore undiscovered creature. Her neck looks exposed. My eyes are drawn to her waist. Normally, I don't dwell on physical appearances, but with the silence between us and the blank biographical canvas it's all I have.

I try and smile.

"You're Erica." *Stupid*. She knows her own name. She nods slowly.

"I, uh...." Fuck. "I like your eyes."

In hindsight, the silence that came before her piercing wails of derisive laughter was almost blissful. Potential hanging on a knife edge, waiting to either draw away or slice me open. I run back to my cabin and spend the night clutching my stomach.

XI

At 7PM, two and a half hours after executing Peter Garforth at a crowded fundraiser, I close the door to my apartment and lock the door. I know immediately that someone else is here - security line broken, different scent, blinds half a centimeter higher than they were when I left - but I still feign surprise when I switch on the light and see him sitting in the lounge, glass in his hand, looking every bit as young as he was ten years ago.

Okay. I'm a little surprised. But something followed me home. Some *omen*. In a city where everything is perfectly tuned, exactly designed to produce an exact psychological response, you can tell when something's off-kilter. Or I can tell. He motions for me to sit down.

The tension in the room could be sliced with a scalpel.

Finally, he sighs.

"I'm thinking I might retire," he murmurs, setting his glass down. I'm not sure if he's talking to me, or himself. "If that's possible, I mean. Just... find somewhere quiet. Somewhere I don't have to deal with *people*." With that word, he shoots me a dirty look.

I shrug. "Hasn't hurt me. Not dealing with people is what I do best." I offer a smile. He doesn't take it.

"You - no, sorry. You definitely deal with people. Just

because the way you do it is through occasional explosions of violence, rather than the ordinary interactions of everyone else, that doesn't mean you're not dealing with them. You heard of the butterfly effect?"

I nod. "Sure. Every sci-fi flick about time travel tries to shoehorn it in. Go back in time to kiss the girl you had a crush on, accidentally create nuclear Armageddon." I had watched that one a couple of years ago.

He rolls his eyes. "Right. Except we *know* the future." There's a pause. "OK, no, we don't. That's stupid. But we have a decent approximation of it, and as long as... *you lot* don't fuck things up, the amount of re-calculation stays fairly small. We can adjust, and keep everything in balance. Like - okay, here's an example I heard about a few weeks ago. Some desk clerk in the financial district discovers that he has business savvy far beyond his station. His fulfilment plan involves him finding personal bliss through other means, but all of a sudden he decides he's going to write a *book* about succeeding in business. And then, against all odds, this *book* ends up attracting a lot of fans and he becomes a full-time motivational speaker with a much cushier lifestyle than he was ever supposed to get."

He looks a little red-faced. I can't tell if it's the exertion of explaining himself, or the empty glass of Scotch in his hand. I shrug.

"So? Good for him."

"Right - except that means that, uh, CAIN has to run a shitload of calculations - we're talking billions here, not exactly an aptitude test in mental arithmetic. Sorry. Uh. A shitload of calculations, so that everyone else can attain a meaningful life without this fucker screwing it all up. And it's manageable! Everyone keeps on keeping on, and while you might have the odd outage as it sources a little more processing power, everything remains more or less unchanged."

By this point, I think I know what's coming.

"But killing a high-profile figure who wasn't supposed to be killed... that's fucking... that's fucking *huge*, you know?" He fixes me with an alarmingly sober glare. "Check your specs."

At this point, I realize that I haven't checked them all day. I silence everything as a matter of routine prior to kills, purely for the sake of focus - having half-minute bulletin updates roll in as I'm trying to line up a shot is infuriating. I slide my thumb over the rim and it hums into life. I don't need to read the backlog to get the gist.

```
GARFORTH NO LONGER -
RETURN TO -
PAYMENT AS NORMAL -
URGENT: ACKNOWLEDGE   RECEIPT   OF
UPDATE THAT TARGET IS NOT PETER-
```

"Sorry, but this has put us in a - well - *very* awkward situation."

And then - well, we already went over this, right? There weren't any cuffs, but my apartment already felt oppressive. I remember being indignant and screaming once he introduced the Exile Kit, but I was probably a lot calmer. Maybe I spoke through gritted teeth, or maybe I sympathized. For a few minutes back there, I felt like we both shared a sense of being out of place. He would have loved this colony, I think.

I never got his name. I feel like I should have asked.

XII

"You've stopped staring."

I snap out of my usual trance, a daily blank state precision-cutting circuit boards and allowing everything else to fade out. Standing next to me is someone I think I've seen near my unit. She might be a construction worker - or maybe she's laying phone lines. She's smiling, and well-built, but not in any obvious way - it's a general impression, rather than the buxom outlines you used to see glowing from skyscrapers.

"Staring?"

"Every day, I walk past, and your hands are working, but you're staring at the city. Not today. Decide you like the job?" I look up. It's still there, shining through the heat, a mirage. For the first few weeks, I kept looking back at it. I don't like the job, but it means that I get to stay. It affords me the privilege to access books I didn't know existed, to eat well, and to enjoy a strange sort of peace. I gesture at the delicate circuitry in front of me, and shrug.

I'm suddenly aware that my cheeks are hot. It's hard to process what this means. She breaks the awkward pause.

"Anyway, I, uh... I saw the book you're reading. I won't spoil it for you, but, ah...." She breaks off, looking agitated.

"What?" She grins at me.

"You're in for a treat, that's all I'll say. You read a lot?" I nod. I'm not sure where this is going, but at the same time I'm not sure I mind. The usual pained awkwardness is missing. "We should swap recommendations - I've been on a roll for the last few weeks. Want to meet once you're done with work?" This stuns me. It really *is* a hot day. My cheeks are burning.

"Oh! No." *What?* She looks pensive, and begins to turn away. "I mean yes. Yes!" The smile comes back, and with it, a strange sense - fear, maybe, but tied up with something else.

XIII

Eighteen.

The door's open. Just a crack - just enough to let me know that it's unlocked. I walk over, shut it, then fall back into my cot.

A few seconds later, there's a small electronic squeal and the door opens again.

I don't want to go. I'm gripped by anxiety - not the dramatic, wide-eyed kind, but the kind that paralyses you and makes everything seem insurmountable.

The funny thing is, there's so much that I'm looking forward to. The simplicity of a clean bullet to the head of someone who needs it - and by *needs it*, I mean a personal need, not a need judged by the media or a mass of blank faces. A nicer apartment, with quieter neighbors and a stronger sense of security. Information networks that never suffer from outages.

But it's what I have to do to get to that point. I have to travel across a bustling metropolis, and sign up for a job that I'll never go to. That means ticket inspectors, strangers in the street, tax officers, employment assessors, and a whole host of unknown values that I'm not ready for. I sit with my back to the door, pressing it shut, and that same squeal rings out, this time rising in a crescendo until I back off again.

I grab my things. It all fits into one bag. I could hear others packing long into the night, talking in hushed, excited voices. It only made me feel worse. Ninety per cent of the time, that sense - of other people having a better handle on all of it - goes unnoticed, because they're other people. I don't want to be them. Sometimes, it grates, though. It's like an itch that I can't quite reach, because I'm not quite sure where it is.

The door swings open. I feel like I'm being watched. I probably am. I step out, and deliberately turn left, even though access to the surface is the opposite direction. Every other cabin in the corridor is empty, the lights dimmed, covers strewn everywhere. A canteen has been thrown to the floor, the name *ERICA* harshly scratched into the side. A pair of panties lies in another room. Something terrifying and unknown briefly stirs in me, and I look away quickly before it develops. In every room, there are more mementos. A necktie. A blue shirt, and a glimmer of metal poking out from the corner that suggests handcuffs. I don't question any of it. I just take it in, absorbing the silence.

There's a door at the end, but with no discernible way of getting through. I press my ear to it, and think I can hear voices, but with the upstairs access letting in the noise of the city, I could just be hearing things. I breathe in, close my eyes, and turn on my heel. The sooner this is over, the better.

XIV

After my face is plastered on every billboard in the city, and the public get the show trial they never knew they wanted, the gates to the city close behind me. There are two turrets, waiting for the slightest sign of rebellion. I start walking away.

I make the Exile Kit last.

In front of me is dust. Apparently, in other countries, there was no Great Levelling - rather than grinding everything into the land, the ruins of cities stand as warnings to visiting creatures from far-off galaxies. Here, though, part of the preparation was to vaporize every structure, to turn it all into dirt, and use the microbial remnants to synthesize new matter. In front of me, there's nothing. Already, it feels cold. I pull my jacket around me a little tighter and start walking.

A modified synthesizer sits in my pack, along with about seven kilograms of gel cubes, waiting to unpack and re-arrange their molecules. It's all woefully unhelpful - death row feasts, not sustainable nutrition. This one becomes a beef burger on a seeded bun. This one, a bowl of ramen noodles. A milkshake. A packet of chips. Nothing designed to keep me going more than a month. But I make it last.

Water is a harder one to solve. I have the equipment for saving rainwater, which is supposed to be safe to drink again, but I'm left to the whims of the weather. It's storm season, though. For at least a month, I end up lucky, but my clothes stink of stagnant water.

The food runs out. I keep walking until I can't, and then I crawl. More than once, I inch past skeletons frozen in a similar pose. I wonder about deviating from the same path, but then wonder what the point would be. When I die, at least I'll have the company of other bones.

"Dead?"

XV

Back in the city, two years ago, music blares from every corner of my apartment - a deep, thrumming bass that eases me out of my usual alert state. I'm reading about Tangier in the 1960s. The rumor was that North Africa degenerated before anyone could agree on a consensus. Hard to tell. The telecoms infrastructure was the first thing to fall.

It doesn't matter, though, because in my mind's eye people are retreating into illicit dens where alcohol and hashish are passed around. Hushed tones. An electric, erotic frisson hanging in the air, threatening to take shape into something unspeakable and scandalous. Somehow, the perfect balance between darkness and light, underneath the hot evening air and the call to prayer from a hundred mosques.

I love reading about this sort of thing. Speakeasies in the 1920s. Teenagers at the turn of the 21st century, retreating to suburban parks to get stoned. Brothels on the outskirts of Las Vegas, as if flung in embarrassment from the heart of the city. I've noticed that there's a smirk that develops on my face when I read about this sort of thing. Intoxication by proxy. Lust, not quite containing itself.

It takes me a second to notice that I've sprung to my feet. Why? I narrow my eyebrows. Instinct appears to have kicked in. It's only as I'm dressing myself that I realize I'm preparing to go out. To a club, or a bar, or a place where someone might look at me with a subversive but thrilling agenda rather than just casual friendliness.

As soon as I attach coherency to the thought, the insecurity steps in. I wake my specs and scan the latest bulletins. *Riots.* I put down my keys. *Thirty arrests.* My coat slides off. *Two fatal stabbings at a nightclub.* Shoes, socks. *General civil unrest.* I fall, emotionally exhausted, into bed.

Maybe another night.

XVI

The first time we try anything, I panic and tell her to leave. The second, I don't. Recommending books is easy. This is something different.

I'd read about a lot of romances. Push-pull feelings of jealousy, deaths, farces, and the sort of behavior behind closed doors that made me squirm whenever I read it. But they were all fictional. Dealing with a living, breathing woman with her hand between your legs is something very different. Exciting, but terrifying too. The constant feeling that you're going to do something wrong. The occasional revulsion that someone else is in your immediate vicinity.

The anxiety from this new life still hits me in waves, but there's something I can't fathom that pushes me on. Maybe it's the knowledge that I have to leave for work every day, otherwise I won't eat. On some days, a job like that is just uncomfortable. On others, it's intolerable. But as the days turn to weeks, and the weeks to month, the panic subsides, and eventually the prickling discomfort fades to monotony.

No - wait - monotony doesn't cover it. Because the first day I come home and realize I've had a boring day at work, I *shriek* with happiness. I punch the air like a schoolgirl. I sit down, and a wave of euphoria washes over me. I can't explain it, but it feels nothing like finishing a book, or executing a particularly clean kill, or making it home without seeing another soul - those experiences leave me with a sense of contentment, but nothing like this.

Only after the boredom became normal did she come along. I wonder how I'd have dealt with her a month before.

The first time we spoke, it felt like my throat was sealed shut. Rather than talk at length, I'd scroll through my specs, point out titles to her, and look animated while she enthused about a particular genre or style. For the first week, I probably said no more than a couple of dozen words. But again, I went home happy. I wasn't silent out of discomfort. We were finding a dynamic - or rather I was, and she was gleefully flowing around it. I would begin to talk more, and she would talk less. I would rest a hand on her shoulder, waiting for her to snap, and she would move a little closer, or rest her hand on mine. Day by day, we would shed inhibitions so glacially that it was hard to notice what constituted a major shift until we were naked, side by side, taking it in turns to burst into fits of giggles.

Hard to make sense of all of this.

She was wrong - I do still look back at the city, that glimmering empire with a perfect place for almost everyone. I wonder how exactly that perfection is designed. How a series of algorithms could create the most eloquently-lived life with 100% accuracy in the first place. I wonder about Erica, the girl who laughed. About a city that always seemed spotless and peaceful until viewed through the lens of the media. About lives blinked out for the greater good. About the illusion of freedom. About the man in my apartment, the empty glass in his hand.

I think about the fight over food I stumbled across two nights ago, and how the man who died for the sake of a synthetic loaf of bread had nothing but disappointment in his eyes as he faded to black. About the brutal punishment for the perpetrator. About senseless violence, but also the strange capacity to run away from it at all costs, knowing that it won't catch up to you if you run fast enough. About the phrase "coming into your own". About the groove between her collarbone and her neck, and the way she sometimes laughs for no reason, as if she can't contain her happiness. About arbitrary limits to potential. About a limitless life.

A SILENT AMPHITHEATER

Before

The hood comes off, the immobilizer still thrumming with energy. Only when the footsteps recede and the door seals shut does it deactivate. Every wall is white. The silence is eerie. So much *noise* - the low rumble of the police transport, the metallic thud of a door blasting off its hinges, a thousand watchers with muffled voices. Only now is there some respite. He scratches the itch on his neck that had been building for hours. Runs his fingers through his hair. Greasy, streaked with dirt. Blinks.

Geraldo Casales.

There is no point of origin, as if the voice - a woman, sounding impossibly flat, a heartbeat away from robotic - is seeping through every pore in the room. No echoes. As if the voice is in his head. He wonders if that's the point.

"Where am I?"

You have been named a suspect regarding the death of

Ruari Simonstone. You do not have to say anything, but anything you do will be recorded and used to inform the judicial process. Please confirm your understanding of this statement.

"... I understand." It's hard to judge the tone in his voice. Resignation, maybe. Or just tiredness. It's a while before the voice comes back. This time, he thinks he can detect a flicker of uncertainty, or something close to it.

At this point, you will be offered a choice. You may be tried by means of the exclusive efforts of CAIN and its field representatives, with no right to appeal. If found not guilty, you will be released and compensated. If found guilty, you will face exile. Please confirm your understanding of this option.

A nod. They *must* be watching him.

You may also be tried under the court of popular opinion. You will be required to testify before one thousand remote jurors. You must answer any and all questions asked of you. Evidence will be presented before the jurors, if deemed relevant. Any question may be asked up to three times and on three separate occasions; you may answer identically each time, or change your response. Your fate will be decided by simple majority vote based on the strength of your testimony, with no right to appeal. If found not guilty, you will be released and compensated.

The next sentence sounds forced. As if the person reading it is doing so for the first time.

If found guilty, you will be publicly executed by hanging from the neck until dead, no less than seven days after the verdict. Please confirm your understanding of this option.

Another nod.

His mind is already made up.

Day One

A thousand citizens are sat at desks across the city, while instructions fade in.

Leaving the trial will incur a penalty and the depreciation of your vote.

There will be multiple recesses throughout the day.

You may discuss the defendant's guilt or lack thereof with other jurors using the comments feed. You are required to keep a civil tone.

For an hour, it is stuck in a holding pattern, one static slide juxtaposed against a cheery instructional flick filled with smiling families, an actor decked out in an ill-fitting three piece suit, gesticulating wildly in silent defiance. By the eighth repetition, some jurors get up to use the bathroom, and an alarm bathes the room in a harsh red light. Most sit down again. One or two leave, only coming back hours later. The vast majority, though, feel stuck to their seats. This is something *new*.

Lights, camera -

Within seconds, comments have flooded the right side of the screen. A thousand people making casual guesses as to the identities of other jurors, making conversation. It subsides, though only a little, when Geraldo Casales enters the court. He already looks beaten. An interrogator sits at a desk at his eye level, a wispy goatee and trimmed moustache deliberately distracting from his sunken eyes. He can't be a day past thirty, but the air he gives off is of a man twice his age. Geraldo is in handcuffs, but they are loose enough for him to grasp the glass of water before him and drink, like a man dying of thirst.

Besides the two of them, a water dispenser, two glasses and the desk, the room is empty. Three cameras are trained on the pair. One capturing every facial tic and emotional response from Geraldo, one trained on the desk, and a wide shot of the two. Despite the mass audience, it feels intimate. A trial for public consumption is still just two men in a room.

"Geraldo Casales, I have been appointed to question you about the death of Ruari Simonstone, and gather any contributing testimony as to your moral character. Shall we begin?" Geraldo nods wearily. "Very well. Tell me how you began your day on the first of this month."

Geraldo starts slowly. His voice sounds cracked and brittle. Underused. After a few sentences, the words come more naturally, and he looks up at the inquisitor.

"My day began as any other day does, mister, ah -"

"Tenpenny. Horace." Geraldo looks surprised. It's hard to place, but this thin, angular man does not look like a Horace.

"Mr. Tenpenny, I began my day with the usual routine. I set the automatic livestock care protocols running, sat down to a breakfast of sausage and eggs, and refreshed myself on the stock bulletins."

"You're a farmer, then. Any specialization?"

"Livestock, mostly. Also wheat. Organic produce. None of that synthetic rubbish."

"You'd be referring to the food that eighty-seven percent of the population currently eat."

"That's the stuff." A twinkle flickers briefly in Geraldo's eye, before being extinguished by Tenpenny's exasperated sigh.

"Why stocks?"

"Sorry?"

"You mentioned reading the stock bulletins. You don't strike me as a man desperate to keep up with the banking sector."

"Ah - no - but I deal in luxury commodities, Mr. Tenpenny. Few buy my produce, but the ones who do pay a good price. I need to know if they expect to pay less... or if I can afford to charge a little more. Not that I do. A customer's trust is far more valuable than any single transaction, sir."

Geraldo already looks comfortable. The sweat on his brow has faded. Tenpenny smiles, glad that this job - his first day in practice, though it comes after months of training behind the closed doors of CAIN's experimental social research facility - is going so smoothly so far. No hardballs, yet. They will come later. But comfort is key. Everything else follows. Trust the person asking the questions, and the invisible eyes of a thousand slowly fade away. That's when the confessions bubble up to the surface.

Tenpenny straightens up.

"Now, Geraldo. I want you to cast your mind back to that day. Go through the events in your head. Try and be as confident in your own memory as possible, because I'm going to ask a lot of questions once you're ready. Is that understood?" Geraldo's brow furrows in concentration. He remembers.

*

Birdsong. The aviary was less than a mile away, so the sound of cuckoos always accompanied his breakfast on the porch. It was sweltering, even at this early hour. Forecasts put outdoor temperatures on a steady decline for the next couple of decades before an inevitable plateau, but until then Geraldo had to contend with hot summers and freezing winters.

Memory is hard to keep chronological. He can keep his breakfast isolated, but everything from then on is interspersed with flashes of red. He reads the wind forecast for the next 24 hours. Blood on the walls. A couple of dozen lines of code, tapped through at lightning speed to define the subroutines for the rest of the day. An arm, barely recognizable, the skin flayed off around the circumference, exposing muscle fiber and bone, already gathering dust and flies. The low rumble of the hooves of cattle making their way across the field. A skull, cracked, the brain pulped but two brilliant green eyes still staring blankly at him.

Paralyzing terror. The corpse of a young boy, shredded into blood-soaked confetti by a grain thresher. A phone. Street lamps. Glaring, steady blue lights.

"Geraldo?"

A slow fade, then everything snaps back to the present. Geraldo looks up, eyes shimmering.

"Sorry."

"First, tell me about the victim. Were you familiar with Ruari Simonstone?"

"His parents, mostly. They lived nearby - two of my best customers, as it happens. Haven't seen them since...." He pauses here, for breath. "They mostly bought eggs and milk. I think they were vegetarians. Ruari would sometimes come along. Cute kid. He - ah -"

The tears, silent and stoic, have barely formed before Tenpenny produces a pack of tissues from his inside pocket and hands one to Geraldo. The mood feels fragile. Like despair could shift to rage in the space of a second. It only diffuses when Geraldo takes the tissue, dabs at his eyes, and opens them again with renewed focus.

"I knew him fairly well by association. The way you know the kids of any family friends, but there was nothing special there. He - he didn't deserve this." That last sentence feels thick and clumsy, his tongue struggling around the words.

Tenpenny nods. His eyes flicker as he scans his talking points. He smiles, not quite sadly enough as to appear tactful.

"So. Tell me about the equipment connected to Ruari's death. I trust you understand how it works?"

"Yes. It's. Um. Deliberately retrofitted - you feed grain into a cylinder, then start the engine, and the blades inside spin and separate the stalks from the husks. There are a couple of extra steps to remove excess straw and chaff, but... I'm guessing that part's not what interests you." Silence hangs in the air. "If your hand gets stuck, the blades rotate, you're pulled in, torn apart and crushed."

"If? Based on the evidence at the crime scene, that's exactly what happened."

"That's why we have safety checks, though. There's an electromagnetic shield surrounding the machine, as well as a remotely-activated safety barrier that detects human DNA and immediately shuts everything down. Someone would have had to sabotage the shield and hack into my systems to allow this to happen. I mean, someone *did*. I just don't know how."

"You were sabotaged?"

"Look at my file." Tenpenny expands the document for the viewers at home. "This tracks any disturbance to my equipment. At 2:34pm, both the thresher, safety barrier and shields were disabled by an EMP blast at the perimeter of my property. A few minutes later, someone manually reactivated the thresher at the scene. I assume Ruari."

"Where were you around then?"

"Taking a nap. Nothing usually happens after lunch."

"Do you regret that nap, now?" Tenpenny looks painfully neutral. Geraldo looks right at him, obviously hurt.

"I regret the whole day, Mr. Tenpenny. That doesn't mean it was my fault."

"Why would Ruari go to all this trouble to get to a thresher?"

The pause this time swells slowly, like a balloon continuing to inflate far beyond its capacity.

"I... don't know. There might have been an accomplice. Theoretically, if you had large quantities of cannabis leaves, you could alter the machine to grind it down, but even that seems like a stretch. By large, I mean tons. He didn't strike me as a wholesaler. Ruari was only fifteen."

"So - when did you discover him?"

"About three. It took a little while for me to gather myself."

"You called the emergency services at 4:30."

"I was in a state of shock. Someone had been shredded to pieces on my property." Geraldo sounds curiously flat, now, as if any display of emotion might break him.

"Very well. To confirm, though - you don't hold yourself responsible?"

"Look. I don't know what you usually do, Mr. Tenpenny, and I'd never complain about my income, but my job is *rough*. I run a 24-hour operation. Yes, it might be principally automated, but livestock have a habit of defying automation. I have birthed animals using my bare hands. I have had to slaughter creatures myself because the city diverts my power to CAIN's data centers once a month. I contend with blistering heat, and debilitating cold, and I do all of this by myself."

"You aren't married?"

"I was. My wife and daughter passed away a couple of years ago."

"I'm sorry." Geraldo looks angry, but he relents a little at this. His face softens.

"Yeah... me too."

"Your fingerprints were found on the threshing machine. And on the boy's body."

"It's my machine. And I panicked. I think part of me thought that he could be saved."

"Really? He was... scattered."

Geraldo's eyes are red. The atmosphere feels heavy.

"Let's resume this tomorrow." To no-one, Tenpenny enunciates clearly and crisply. "End of testimony number one." The feed cuts to static.

Night One

"Put this on."

Everything has been more relaxed since Geraldo agreed to a public trial. His cell is more of a break room, with a sofa, a twin bed, and a few neural downloads on the table. He still has no idea where he is - packed with home comforts it might be, but it's windowless, giving him the impression that he's marooned on a distant space station, or in some strange version of purgatory. Which, when he thinks about it, he sort of is.

The guard hands over specs and Geraldo reluctantly takes them. He prefers to *read* - rather than controlling the endless stream of information with a focused mind, he likes to touch, to watch the words glide under his fingertips. He accepts it without a struggle, though. Everyone is being so *courteous*, but there's an unspoken accord that if he makes things difficult, they can choose not to be.

At midnight, the lights suddenly black out. He isn't sure, but far off somewhere he thinks he can hear alarm bells.

And then:

"Oh-my-god. Noooo. Really? I really did it? WOW."

Geraldo's specs flicker into life, the cool blue glow accompanying the sound of a girl's voice. By her enthusiasm, and her inflection, she can't be much older than eighteen.

"Okay so, um, just to check - you *are* Geraldo, right? Because I tried something like this last week and now some old dude in his forties won't stop calling me. How was I to know? I thought "sugar daddy" meant something *completely* different, okay?"

"Huh?" Geraldo's eyes flicker open. Underneath the door, he can see a flashing red light. "Who is this?"

"Oh. Yeah." She laughs, but it's free from scorn, sounding more bemused than dismissive. "I'm... May. Sorry, I just *had* to speak to you. You fucking weirdo. Is that rude? Sorry, that's probably rude. You're not saying anything."

"I mean..." he pinches his brow. "Why are you talking to me? Surely this is illegal?" There's a pause, where she ums and ahs for a few seconds. He can almost see the look of concentration on her face.

"Yeah, I suppose it is. Hadn't thought of that. Seriously, though, I left a hole in their security infrastructure so big that it's gonna take them *hours* to fix it. So - how are ya, Geraldo? And is Casales *really* your last name? Because if it is, it's *perfect*. Really getting the rustic vibe."

"I'm in a prison cell, potentially on the way to my death. How do you think I'm feeling?"

"OH! Yeah - *that's* what I was going to ask you about.

Fuck. Could have reminded me. Yeah - so - Ruari."

Hot, red flashes.

"What about him?" Geraldo's voice is sharpened steel.

"Why'd you lie, man? Ruari was a fucking sociopath. Used to sneak into the girls' locker room and piss in their shoes. One time - you're not gonna believe this - I hear he fucking *branded* a guy. So why'd you say he was, wait, lemme find it -" he can hear a few ferocious taps, then his voice echoes into his ears. *Cute kid*. The words sound strange to him. "I mean, yeah, I guess he has that sleek, I'll kiss you goodnight then slash your throat look to him, or as much as any teenager could, but *dude*. *No-one* liked him. Even his parents were looking to send him away to the factory district. Happens to some of the first-generation surface kids, I guess - no proper values, or whatever. So yeah, anyway, don't let me get distracted again - *why*?"

The words ring in his ears. He keeps trying to form thoughts, but they're just ghosts, flickers of coherency turning to dust. He wonders if this is what a mental breakdown feels like, and if it is, when he can expect to burst into tears.

Maybe he's exhausted, is what he thinks. A day of constant deductive thinking, aggressively analyzing every motivation, picking apart fuzzy memories - maybe this is normal. But he tries to picture Ruari, and finds that he can't. The parents, similarly, turn up a blank. *Something simpler*. Home. Crudely-drawn houses flash up - the drawings of a child - but nothing he can identify with. He closes his eyes, and he's drowning in a bathtub of blood and viscera. He can hear screaming. Wailing. Hysterics. Insistent, annoying, children -

"Ger-*al*-do?"

Everything snaps back, elastic. May is still there. He groans. Pain shoots through his abdomen, like someone has thrown him into a bout of indigestion without warning.

"Oh. Good. Thought I'd lost you there. So, uh, I've gotta go. But this was fun? Don't you like how we can talk like this? I, uh - no, maybe I shouldn't say that."

Geraldo sighs, stretching and standing up. The lights are flickering back on. "What?"

"I just - I figure you're probably pretty lonely. My family died too, you know. I know what it's like."

And then the glow vanishes in an instant. The door bursts open, and seven guards in flak jackets look upon a man whose eyes have seen a little too much.

Day Two

"A drink, you say."

The comments are unusually quiet this morning. The occasional jester shows up, trying to twist the grotesque into something more palatable, but otherwise the torrent has become a trickle. A thousand people are glued in front of a thousand screens, rapt and silent.

"Geraldo - you're aware that this flatly contradicts your earlier statement, that you began the day with a breakfast of... sausage and eggs, was it?"

"Could you repeat that for the record, please?"

Geraldo looks up. His eyes look black, his mouth a thin line.

"I said, get used to it."

Tenpenny's face contorts. He's used to building up a rapport, evolving over time, but this man seems altogether closed off. Something's up.

"Alcoholic, I suppose."

"Yup."

"And do you usually start your day with a drink, Geraldo?"

"Yup."

"... and why is that? I'd assume it steels you for the day ahead, but your work is, ah - largely automated, you said?"

When Geraldo next speaks, it might just be the dense, echoless room, but every word is flecked with venom.

"Until it goes wrong, yes. I mentioned this yesterday: have you ever birthed a calf?" Tenpenny looks taken aback.

"No, I can't say I have."

"It's messy. It stinks. You can smell pain, you know. And that's just the tip of the iceberg. I'm working with a fecal scatterer seven years out of date, and I don't even want to count the number of times it's broken down. If you're spreading shit on the ground with your bare hands just so you can feed yourself, a drink fucking helps."

Tenpenny strokes his goatee, an affectation that (for those who already know the man) betrays an uncommon occurrence - his being lost for words, unable to open his mouth until his mind catches up to the words of his opponent. He does it because he thinks it makes him look refined. To those who know him, and a good portion of the jury, he looks nervous.

"So, ah -" for a moment, it feels like he has forgotten the name of the accused - "Geraldo - why lie during your first testimony? Granted, repeat occurrences like this are designed to weed out the truth, but rarely so dramatically. What changed?"

Geraldo shakes his head.

"I'm sorry?"

"I don't have an answer for that one."

Tenpenny closes his eyes. He looks up, at one of the blinding white walls, crosses his arms over his chest, and the feed pauses. A scarlet message flashes up in every juror's home.

TEMPORARY RECESS: REMAIN IN YOUR SEATS

"Immobilizer." Tenpenny's voice is less patient, now - closer to the title of interrogator than his usual therapeutic self. The legs of Geraldo's chair snap apart, the plastic melding into a new shape, humming faintly as it locks Geraldo in place. "Don't worry. Just a precaution." He nods, and in steps a man with an air of *much* higher authority. He wears a fitted black jumpsuit, his shoulders broad and proud. Old, but not lacking strength - an eighty-year-old battle-axe with piercing blue eyes and a grave voice that makes Geraldo feel very small. He offers no introductions.

"Geraldo Casales. This break in the trial has come because of your refusal to continue. You will be asked a series of yes or no questions in order to establish a lack of corruption and your further compliance. This is not being recorded, as it does not form part of your testimony regarding the crime in question. If you are found to be lying, you will be sentenced to exile with no right of appeal. Understood?"

"... yes."

"Good." The man's voice rings in his ears. "Of these individuals," he barks, opening up a reader and scrolling through sixteen expressionless faces, "do you know or have you met any outside trial proceedings?" One of the faces is of a teenage girl, all dreadlocks and lip piercings, looking as if she's desperately containing a smirk.

"No."

"Were you in anyway culpable for the power cut that lasted from between midnight and 2am on today's date, the thirteenth of July?"

"No."

"Since your incarceration, have you been provided with any information of which you were not already aware?"

Geraldo tries to think. He looks hollow, strapped up like this. Finally, after deliberating -

"No."

The man fixes him with a glare that lasts all of ten seconds. Geraldo can hear his heart thrumming in his chest. Finally, he sighs.

"Very well." He nods at Tenpenny. "Continue."

He leaves, and the feed resumes.

"Strike the previous question from the record. Geraldo has established with sufficient credibility that he has no suspect grounds upon which to provide an altered testimony, and that any new comments have arisen from further personal deliberation." He nods, seemingly to himself, proud of his concision. It all seems a bit forced.

"You said yesterday that you live alone on the farm. Can you confirm this?"

"Yes, that's correct."

"And your wife and child are -"

"Dead. Yes."

"Were you personally familiar with Ruari Simonstone?"

There is a beat before Geraldo answers.

"No."

"No?"

"No."

"You had never met him prior to the day of his death?"

"I met him, but I wasn't personally familiar with him. You're not personally familiar with the people you see on the street, are you?"

"Ah - so you had encountered him, but nothing more?"

"Correct."

"I want to talk a bit more about your business, Geraldo. What do you farm, exactly?"

"Cattle, mostly."

"That's presumably for milk?"

"And meat, and leather." Tenpenny wrinkles his nose at this.

"There's demand for that?"

"No - but the people who pay, pay well. I only need a few customers a month to keep me going." He senses Tenpenny's next question by the revolted look on his face. "They're killed humanely. Yes, it's grotesque if you're used to zapping gel cubes - I stun them, and bleed them dry - but less grotesque than burning two thirds of this continent's livestock alive for the sake of what you types like to call 'structural benefit'. I provide authenticity, Tenpenny. A sense of the natural way of things. Can you say you do the same?"

"With all due respect, Geraldo, this testimony is designed to shed light on *your* -"

"I thought as much." Geraldo's lips curl into a sneer, suddenly full of disdain for the man in front of him. Tenpenny clears his throat - a little nervously, it seems.

"So you're familiar with the Great Levelling."

"Don't patronize me, sir. I wanted to work on the land since I was a kid. You have to know your options if you're coming up to an earth that's utterly alien to you. I would have preferred sheep, but some bright spark decided that wool was an, uh - what do you types call it? – 'Priority Three Product'. Slaughtered them all in less a month. You want to argue about ethics, try and justify that."

"Was Ruari killed in your crop shredder?"

"Yes. Nothing else could have done that to him."

"Is it your fault?"

But the words *so you're familiar with the Great Levelling* are still ringing in Geraldo's ears, and for a moment he just sits there, numb. There is some part of his frantic, anguished, furious mind that wants to scream out, but right now it's buried under some awkward restructuring process. Shards of memory are being carefully extracted, worn down until the fungus is swept away, then carefully replaced. It's so haphazard. Geraldo can feel his temples pounding as his subconscious works twice as hard. He keeps thinking about that girl.

What am I missing?

He starts, then bites his lip. He knows that the way he currently looks, it must give the impression that he's about to lie, but really he's just trying to think of something to say that will fit when he works out the truth. If. So:

"No."

"... end of testimony number two."

Night Two

>*So - how're you gonna play this?*

The words flicker across Geraldo's specs. He can hear cooling fans and muttering somewhere behind closed doors.

"You again."

>*Say that a bit louder. I think there are a few exiles who didn't hear you.*

He rolls onto his side, his eyes half-lidded, and mumbles. He thinks that by doing this, he won't be found out. He is -

astoundingly - right.

Can't risk another blackout. Cops get wise to repeat patterns. Had to go for stealth. You looked a fucking mess today, you know.

"... thanks."

>*You're welcome. You didn't answer my - wait, was that sarcasm? You know you're just being transcribed, right? That wasn't very nice.*

"Mhm." Geraldo stretches his legs. He isn't sure why she decided to come back.

>*I'm thinking you did it. Like. It just makes sense.*

"Don't be stupid. I don't care if he was a maniac - I don't just kill kids, you know." Radio silence. "Those stories about hick farmers abducting and dismembering children are a bit cliché." Still nothing. Then:

>*Your memory isn't too hot, is it? I can tell.*

HOT. Flames lick at the walls. He can hear screaming, laughing, the smell of bacon. Charred corpses. Running. Running for who? The heat on his back. Tears streaming down his face. Ruari. The sound of a match being struck. Sniggering. A collapsing beam, sparking hot, bashing in the brains of his daughter. Ruari Fucking Simonstone. Turning, falling, every breath gone from his body. The barn, twice the size of the house, burning to the ground, a huge funeral pyre for his wife and daughter. Fumbling with his specs in the corn.

And then, other things. Things he knows now, but can't yet put words to. Tears fog up the headset. He can see words frantically being typed out. He blinks back the tears.

>*Hey. Uh. Say something. You're freaking me out.*

"Who are you?"

Now it's her turn to be silent. Finally, after a few

minutes, when he's about to drift off into an unfulfilling sleep, a single line scrolls into view.

>*You did the right thing.*

Day Three

"I hope you slept well, Geraldo. Moment of truth, this." Tenpenny licks his lips - or rather, his tongue darts out surreptitiously, catching an errant crumb in his moustache. He looks especially well-groomed today - his goatee is combed to a fine tip, and Geraldo can see the barest trace of hair wax lingering in his eyebrows. He has almost forgotten that a thousand people are watching, ready to decide his fate at the push of a button.

"Let's get this over and done with." Geraldo sounds more measured today. The darkness is gone in his voice, replaced by something more mournful. Still, the thing that comes out is a sense of balance. No more sweating, racing pulse; but, by the same token, it looks for the first time like the man sitting there is real.

"Very well." Tenpenny clears his throat. "Starting at the beginning, then. You began your day -"

"With a drink. Of scotch. Unhealthy, but sometimes necessary in my line of work. That probably makes me an alcoholic, I know, but there are times where the prospect of another day by myself is too much to deal with while sober."

"Have you sought help? For your addiction, I mean."

"No." Geraldo looks at his feet, his mouth twisted in concentration. "Perhaps I should. I guess I haven't really given it much thought."

"Sorry." It's out of Tenpenny's mouth before he can retract it, and the word disturbs him. He pushes past it, as if rushing out the next question can erase anything preceding it. "Tell me how you came to be alone."

"I used to have a wife and a daughter. A group of kids led by Ruari blew up the old barn on my property while they were trapped inside, and they burned to death. You can still see the blast marks from the old building if you look."

An invisible audience is slack-jawed with shock.

"That's... quite an accusation. Were there any witnesses?" Tenpenny regrets it before he's even finished the line.

"No. Sadly, no. I wouldn't be here if there were. But I think we both know that, Mr. Tenpenny."

Dread fills the room. Time slows. Geraldo himself has only just worked out how to admit the next part, and he does it without being prompted.

"So I planted a seed. Ruari was at the farm with his parents. They were picking up a dozen eggs. I told them that I needed to get them some change from the safe, but that they were welcome to follow me. I could feel Ruari's eyes on my back when I was taking their money. He was leaning against the threshing machine every time. The next four visits, I did exactly the same. I filled the safe with blank notes."

"You still operate a cash business?"

"A lot of us do out in the sticks, Mr. Tenpenny. Solar flares interfere more if you don't have skyscrapers blocking the view. The point is, Ruari was getting interested. He thought I was rich."

Geraldo looks blank. In truth, every emotion had shot through his body hours earlier, lying in his cot, as the memories slammed themselves against the walls of his skull. He had buried his face in his pillow and screamed his guts out. Now, all of this feels like a poor facsimile. Still genuine, but from a place of emotional exhaustion rather than hysteria.

"I set up a silent trip alarm, so that when Ruari stepped on to my property in the dead of night I would know. I walked out into the yard and strangled him. And then I fed him into the threshing machine to hide my fingerprints."

Tenpenny frowns. He feels a little redundant. This was supposed to be his crowning achievement - breaking the unbreakable man - and he has the distinct impression that his subject already arrived in pieces. He probes, nevertheless, trying to find some hidden mystery.

"Why hide if you were going to confess later?"

"I had no idea what I was going to do after he was dead. Never confuse a thorough plan with a long-term view. It's fairly common knowledge that people contemplating suicide are disproportionately proficient when it comes to deductive reasoning as far as doing the deed, but give little thought to how and when they might be discovered. I wanted to kill him - I wanted revenge - but I hadn't really thought about anything following that."

"O-OK, but why a *threshing machine* of all things?"

Geraldo smiles humorlessly.

"I thought the greater the sense of catastrophe, the more satisfying it would feel."

"And did it?"

Geraldo sighs. He knows he doesn't have to say anything else. All he has to do now is await the inevitable.

Night Three

"Get up."

Geraldo recognizes the guard as one of the men who was

pointing a gun at him on the night of the blackout. He looks pissed off. Geraldo swings his legs out of the cot. He's in no rush.

"No chance of a last meal, I suppose."

"Specs." The guard's meaty palm is outstretched. Geraldo pulls it off gingerly. It feels like May might be trapped in there. May - was she real, or an invented trigger? It is three in the morning now, but an hour earlier he was dreaming that he was gazing at the smoldering ruins of the barn, whispering "Mayday, mayday" over the phone. Maybe she was just another echo.

"Move."

Tenpenny walks up a narrow corridor. There are windowless doors every few meters. More cells? He can't hear another sound apart from his footsteps and those of the guard behind him. Perhaps they're empty, he thinks. Maybe he was a guinea pig.

Finally, they reach the end of the corridor. The words **CHIEF JUSTICE** are emblazoned above a coat of arms embossed in gold. The guard knocks, and a familiar voice signals them to enter.

Sat behind a desk, in an office so ornately furnished that it makes Geraldo's eyes water, is the man in the fitted black jumpsuit. Mr. Yes-or-No. He smiles, though it appears out of bemusement than friendliness.

"Sit." He gestures at an antique leather armchair. Everything in this room feels ripped from another era. The work of an insane taxidermist - the wings of eagles fused to the head of a badger, an otter with what looks like human arms - litters the shelves. Geraldo tries to tear his eyes away from them.

"Geraldo Casales, I am Chief Justice Henriksen of the Court of Popular Opinion. You have been tried by a jury of a thousand of your peers, and with a majority of five hundred and thirty five you have been found..." The man sighs, shakes his head wearily, and looks right at Geraldo, grimacing. "Not guilty."

Geraldo looks through the window. He can see a transport station. People on their way to work. The first glimmer of sunlight on the horizon, shining through rain.

Day Thirty

"Yo."

She looks younger than he thought - maybe about fifteen, with dark brown bangs hanging loosely in front of her face and a burnt orange coat that looks well-worn. Born on the surface, then. He can make out a small hole in her lip, at one time occupied by a stud.

May looks around at the tombstones. "Jeez, you could have picked a cheerier place to hang out."

Geraldo shakes his head.

"Not hanging out. I'm... I'm done with making new friends for a while. Until I get my head straight, at least."

May strides over, her feet a little too large for legs, giving the impression of a clown striding across a circus arena. She peers down at the two headstones in front of Geraldo - one half the size of the other. A non-committal grunt comes from her throat.

"Yeah, thought as much. Mine were just cremated. I wasn't really sure what to do with them. Uh. You know." She smiles weakly.

"Why'd you help me?"

"Woah - dude - I did *not* think I was helping you. I was just... bored, y'know?" Geraldo raises his eyebrows. "And I was a juror. I mean, you were right in front of me all day. We couldn't even piss without setting off alarms." He shakes his head again, and turns to leave.

"Fine. I did it because it looked like you could use some help. First day? Those guys in the threads were ripping you to *shreds*. Fucked me up. I liked the look in your eye, even when you were lying under oath, but those fuckers were just about ready to execute you. Didn't feel right."

"I didn't need helping."

"Eh, you did."

"Well, I don't anymore."

May looks a little puzzled. She had every intention of forgetting about Geraldo until he called her and asked to meet. A confession like this implies a sense of guardianship she never assumed.

"Uh... good?"

Geraldo looks at his feet. He scrapes a fleck of mud off one boot with the other. "Yeah. Thanks."

"What are your plans, now?"

He sighs, and kicks the dirt next to the nearest tombstone absent-mindedly.

"I still have a job. Customers to feed. The usual."

"And you're okay with that? Just go back to what you were doing before? That's enough for you?"

The longest pause. Then he looks right at her, smiling, only containing the slightest hint of sadness.

"I think so. Yeah." He nods. "That's enough."

Geraldo turns on his heel and makes the journey home.

BLOODTHIRSTY MEDIA

One

"Erica Hazel, eighteen years old, steps out of her room, turns left, and sees a long spiral staircase at the end of the corridor, winding upwards. She - oh, fuck me, not *again*...."

Through bleary, sedated eyes, I could just about make out the shape of two dark-suited grown-ups. There would be a flicker of this in seven years' time, when I reached the surface, stared out at a brilliant sunset that felt strikingly real next to flicks and images, and felt an all-consuming sense of purposelessness. Maybe I'd get a twinge of the unknowable when I curled up in a shop doorway, shrouded in a filthy blanket and ignored by the vast majority - a sense that living day-to-day like that was not what was supposed to happen. Other than that, this would be buried at the bottom of my memory forever.

"You remember orders. Stay calm. Well-intentioned. The guiding hand, remember?" A woman's voice. Fainter.

"There's nothing *here*, though. Must be another network outage," the other voice muttered. A man. As far as I can make out.

"So? Improvise," she said, matter-of-factly.

"Can't we just come back tomorrow? Making something up feels a little dicey." There was a pause, then, followed by an exasperated sigh from the man's partner.

"Did you - fucking hell. This stuff should be second nature to you. You got the same training, right?"

"Mmm."

"We have one shot at this. Any more than that, and it's like lashing out a dog twice - the brain already suspects something's up when you enter the room. Sedation only achieves so much, you know."

"You hit dogs?"

"Clock's ticking."

"Christ. OK." He breathed in sharply. "Erica Hazel, eighteen years old, steps out of her room, turns left, and sees a long spiral staircase at the end of the corridor. You are *filled* with the thrill of a new adventure. You - uh - you have no idea what faces you on the surface, but you relish the prospect of the unknowable. You could be *anything*. Where others face a lifetime of prescription, you have the freedom to tailor your own experience. You absorb the world in a way that no-one else can imagine. As time goes by, more and more of your friends and neighbors help nudge you to a better life, but on that first day you feel like you can do anything." A pause. "We good?"

The two figures stood up, then. The woman stepped hurriedly outside, the man uncertainly following her.

They were right, in a sense. On my first day on the surface, I felt as if there were countless possibilities awaiting me, and kept moving with the promise of the new spurring me on. It took about a week for that impulse to vanish.

Two

He was sharp-suited, slicked-back hair, desperately clutching a high-capacity recorder as if it might spirit itself out of his hands at any moment. He eyed me suspiciously. I shuffled along, clutching my bags. Today's haul was impressive. Smoked salmon, an unbroken bag of carrots, and - because we were at a three-month expiry interval - a slightly ridiculous quantity of chocolate. I stank of garbage. Underneath the skip where I'd found today's haul, I had still encountered the usual weeks-old organic mush, and the smell hovered around me like the aura of nervousness the man seemed to have. I set my bags down, and quickly scribbled down his appearance for my notes. He stopped, and looked at me - more curious now than suspicious. Probably noticing the pen and paper. My specs had stopped working months ago, corrupting years of data with it. Without the money to replace them, I had been strictly manual since then. Cautiously, he walked over to me. I stepped back.

"Hey. It's okay," he said, a sheen of confidence masking his sweat-slicked palms. "I'm just wondering if you can help me."

My eyes darted around. Home was half a mile - I could run for it, but I'd have to leave the food behind. There was a knife concealed in the inside compartment of my jacket, but at that range he would see me going for it. I could see a stun gun in his back pocket. I needed to gauge this situation a little more.

"What do you want?"

He cleared his throat.

"I'm writing a story for the Central Bulletin. Apparently there was an armed robbery here a couple of weeks ago, but, ah -"

This cast him in a different light. He looked lost. Of *course* I knew about that.

"Follow me," I ordered. He looked hesitant.

"It's okay, I - I don't want to be any trouble," he stammered, starting to look a little green. I rolled my eyes, picking up my bags again. Behind my veneer of impatience, there was a quiet thrill at how quickly I'd taken control of the situation.

"*Follow me.*" He closed his mouth this time, and nodded, his eyes darting from side to side.

We got back to the commune. Dusty was in the lounge, his legs on the table. I shoved them off, and walked into the kitchen to dump my stuff.

"Who's the prick?" asked Dusty. He was a welcoming host. I emerged from the kitchen, and tried to give the man an apologetic smile. It came out as a grimace.

"He's a journalist, Dusty. Don't be a cunt." I looked at the man, who was delicately fingering his stun gun. I shook my head. "You didn't tell me your name, did you? And don't touch that again. Dusty's a shithead, but if you hurt him I'll kill you."

The man looked wounded - spend so much time around people who live off getting immediately to the point, and social graces are kind of forgotten. I stabbed around in the dark. "Um. What *is* your name?" I asked. He relaxed a little.

"Mark. Mark Lawrence," he smiled, offering his hand. I shook it gingerly.

"Like me, then. Two names that could be your first. That's, uh... cool." I glanced down at the floor. This felt awkward. "Come upstairs. I think I can help you," I said, scratching my temple. Dusty snorted. I kicked the back of the couch.

We entered my room. I scanned around, then pulled down a note.

> 08-23 17:34: *Two women leave Samwell's Electronics with sealed box of readers (approx. 200 if assumed full). First perp approx. 185cm, broad shoulders, blonde hair in a ponytail, minor facial scarring. Second perp shorter, approx. 165cm, large bust (poss. surgical enhancement).*
>
> 08-24 14:13: *Spoke to manager of Samwell's Electronics. Confirms second perp as Sabina Hasan; first perp as yet unknown. Afraid to alert the Watch, cites personal safety as a concern. No officers on scene. Future Watch intervention unlikely.*

"That's all I've got so far, but -" I turned with the note. Mark was staring at the walls, his mouth agape. I turned back around to follow his gaze. Nothing special.

"This is -" he trailed off, his jaw still slack. I tried to finish his sentence.

"My room?"

"Just - the *information* you have here...." He walked gingerly over to a note pinned by the window with a photograph attached. "No - that can't be - *really?*"

I clicked my tongue against the back of my throat, a habit I'd developed whenever I was feeling impatient. I took the note from him, looking at it. It was an old one.

"Oh. Yeah. Harris Pennyweather. He was the guy who killed those triplets a couple of years back. Never got around to reporting that one."

"That was front page news for *three weeks!*" Mark spluttered. "You're telling me you had proof it was him sitting here all that time?"

I lowered my head, trying to figure out whether he was angry, amazed, or a little of both. Meanwhile, Mark was speaking into his recorder.

"You getting this, Phil?" he said. I looked over.

"Hey, you can't -" I reached out to grab the recorder, or whatever it was, only stopping when it started to speak.

"Yeah. This is... you have to bring this girl in. I'm looking around here and there are stories you morons spent *weeks* trying to uncover. Hey! You!" it barked. Nice. Lovely way to talk to someone in their own home. Mark hesitantly waved the recorder in my general direction. It carried on speaking. "How do you fancy a job, huh? The pay's shit and you have to work with idiots like this guy, but other than that...." He trailed off, but I knew what was left unsaid.

Other than that, you can live in a place where you won't face the threat of forced eviction every day. Other than that, you know where your next meal is coming from - and, incredibly, what it's going to be. Other than that, you can get away from the months of depression that ebb and flow in and out of your life because you're so fucking directionless that obsessively cataloguing everything around you might as well be your chief skill on your resume.

Within a week I got my first headline.

Three

They'd wanted to call him "Mr. Pinprick", which blew my mind, if only for how moronic it sounded. Not that there was anything we could reasonably call him, given that we were completely restricted by *modus operandi*. I can't remember who settled on the Vampire, but after the first mention it stuck. It wasn't perfect, but it was just entertaining enough to keep the public interested without disgusting them.

"What do you have for me, Tim?"

Tim was hovering around the parking garage, looking nervous. There was an unspoken accord between the cops and the press that we just took whatever they gave us and didn't ask questions, but I had leverage on Tim. All old news, now, but I had helped him out before, and now I had the commissioner of the Watch eating out of the palm of my hand. Grudgingly. He slipped me a folder, barely making eye contact.

"Crime scene photos, written reports. I've had to redact one or two things, but it's your guy. Our guy. You know what I mean," he muttered.

I thumbed through. Even a cursory glance yielded the obvious markers. Two pinpricks near a main artery - this time, the wrist. Body drained of blood. And the location - two blocks down, three across. Look at a plan of the city, and the killer was following a geographic pattern. Convenience, probably - a way of not re-treading the same path. It was the one thing we couldn't get to fit the narrative, so we'd left it out of the front page news, but each week he was moving south-east. I winced.

"You okay?"

"Yeah. Something I ate," I said.

"Uhuh. I've gotta get back. Don't -" He looked right at me, if only for a second. "Ah, you know what you're doing."

I did. I knew what I was doing when I got home, set up a

trip wire at my front door, switched off every light, receded into the darkest corner of the room and armed my stun gun. Two blocks south, three blocks east. There were seven houses on my block. No guarantees it would be mine.

Even after preparing, there was still a moment's hesitation before I pulled the trigger. You were already falling, so you probably didn't notice, but had you arrived a few minutes later, I'm not sure I could have done it.

Even after defying my expectations, with your unassuming, skinny frame, tying you up was still a nightmare. I tried to keep things simple - one leg each to a chair leg, and your wrists tied behind your back. It only took half an hour for you to wake up. You were disarmingly calm.

"Are you going to kill me?" you asked. "Huh. Sounds strange coming out of *my* mouth."

It was hard to tell while you were sat down, but you were maybe 185 centimeters tall, greying hair, early fifties but lean. Maybe you exercised, or maybe you were just lucky. Your voice was flecked with bemusement. Even having sat watching you for several minutes, you still didn't fit. Even accepting that I *had* no expectations. You looked like the sort of man I might accidentally flirt with after a couple of drinks, not a crazed killer.

"You don't know who I am, do you?" I said, taking care to enunciate every word. I sounded like a little girl. Clearing my throat, I grabbed my reader and opened the latest edition in front of your face. I pointed to this week's article detailing your exploits. "I wrote this." I swiped across to the previous week. "And this." Again - this time, going back to two months prior. "All of them. I've been tasked to every murder you've committed."

You hung your head.

"I see. You've probably already worked this out, but you know that making you next wasn't deliberate, right? I don't have a... vendetta, or anything."

I nodded.

"Good. I'm not - I don't *do* that." You actually looked a little unsettled, as if something was eating away at you. Finally, you blurted it out. "Murder? That's what you've decided on?"

I looked blankly at you.

"What else could it be? You're literally draining the life from their bodies. That's fairly categorical."

"I'm draining their *blood*. Just their blood. Don't you - ugh, do I really have to spell this out?" My expression didn't change. "I'm a trafficker. I transport blood to clients who pay for it. Well - I transport it to my boss, who moves it to clients," you sighed.

"Your boss?"

"I owe him. It was either a year of indentured servitude or he'd cut off my hands. I play the piano." He smiled apologetically, a sort of what-can-you-do look. "My point is, just calling murder is a bit, uh, opaque. It's not like I *want* to be doing this."

I wrinkled my nose.

"Not sure I can write that angle in, sorry," I said. "It's cute, but it doesn't really work unless I admit to having met you."

"What?"

"I mean, the next time you kill someone."

"... you're just going to let me go?" This threw me. The thought of keeping him in my apartment hadn't crossed my mind - I'd only tied him up to be risk-averse.

"Sure. I mean, yes. Why wouldn't I? Without you, I

don't have a reliable story. You've done wonders for my column centimeters," I said, grinning.

He sighed. The next line sounded unusually timid for a man who was used to the sight of blood.

"You - tonight was supposed to be my last. After the next collection, I'm free to do what I want." He looked at me then, almost a little intimidated. "Assuming you don't report me, that is."

And I'm still not sure why I did what I did next. Maybe it was fear - my job was semi-freelance, after all, and The Vampire had been my big scoop - to see it fizzle out so quickly would at the very least deny me a bonus for the year, and at most put me out of a job and back on the streets during the next creative drought. Fear of losing everything had been building and building, the more secure I got. So:

"How about an alliance?" I asked.

"... an alliance."

"Sure. You show me what to do. I do it in your place until the story's run its natural course. Then we part ways. In return, I don't report you."

"You - huh."

"What?"

"You don't mind killing people?" My brow furrowed. I hadn't really thought about that. This was something I'd already been accused of - when the situation called for pragmatism, morals would be thrown out of the window. Even so, on reflection, it didn't seem all too upsetting. And the trade-offs were... handsome. I shook my head. No, I didn't mind. It wasn't that I liked the idea, but the kindness and moral standing of others had never really done me any good. He sat there, in silence, no longer straining against his ties.

"Then... sure, I guess."

Four

"Okay, now, turn that valve...."

A week later I was flooding apartment 335B of the Nixon Building with a paralytic neurotoxin. Within about three minutes, the occupant would lose all motor function. Within seven, all upper brain processes would cease, leaving about an hour-long window before the brain stem expired. As a way to go, it was pretty painless.

The Vampire was standing next to me in the utility closet. He'd insisted on no names, and given that I was reporting on local mythology rather than gritty urban crime, I was okay leaving it that way. I had his biometric data as a backup, but I hadn't checked his details. No doubt they were forged, anyway. Fingerprint replacement was cheap.

We left the cupboard and walked down the corridor. He signaled for me to attach my respirator, and once it was securely fitted, we entered the apartment, equipment in tow.

She was lying on the couch, perfectly serene. Through the mask, I could hear her breathing, but it wasn't the sound, or the glare from her screen, or the three empty bottles of grain liquor on the table that struck me. Instead, her face, frozen in the same expression forever. Sabina Hasan. Hard to forget her. She looked older than I expected, bags around her eyes, mottled skin on the back of her palms, though it was hard to tell where the self-inflicted injury ended and age began.

The Vampire looked expectantly at me. I realized I was staring at her body.

"Something wrong?" He held his gaze impressively. I

wasn't used to confident men.

"Nah. Just... it's nothing," I whispered.

"You need to understand that you killed her when you flooded the apartment; anything you do now is just an afterthought. You get that, right?"

I looked at him witheringly.

"Yes. I get that."

"Good. Then run the test, like I showed you."

Already, I wasn't confident. The drool on her lower lip, the empty bottles - the filtration equipment could neutralize blood alcohol levels up to a point, but it had its limits. Other intoxicants were hit-and-miss. I tilted her head back, and breathed in.

"Now - the snakebite," he said, rolling his sleeves up.

I blinked.

"The what?"

"It's what we call the apparatus. Two prongs - like a snake's fangs."

"... you realize we nicknamed you the *Vampire*, right?"

He shrugged.

"My slang was here first," he said, eyebrow raised. "Don't complain to me because you invented something incompatible."

I shook my head, and inserted the two needlepoint prongs into her jugular, then turned the vacuum pump to its initial setting.

"You only need to leave it like this for a few seconds," he said quietly. "That should do it." I turned it off, and watched as a series of dials and readings flickered into life. Then, what we were looking for: a small green *OK* at the end of her blood work report. Okay for transfusion, stage effects, smoothies - presumably, anything. "Now. Start slow.

You can increase the vacuum level slowly, but start too hard and it isn't pretty."

I was transfixed. The tubes on the apparatus - I couldn't call it the *snakebite*, fuck - flooded red, and I could already hear Sabina's breathing become shallower. The first spurts hit the bottom of the pouch. I increased the pressure.

There was an odd tranquility to this scene. We sat in silence for a few minutes, watching the bladder slowly fill with blood - A-positive, thirty credits for a hundred mils, one thousand five hundred credits in total. Prior to our arrangement, the Vampire was making half that, half of it payable as his debt. I still hadn't asked why. I wasn't sure I wanted to.

He snapped his fingers - the signal that the neurotoxin had cleared the room at last. It had done its work. I removed my respirator, and adjusted my hair. I felt oddly peaceful. Only the air conditioning as background noise. Until:

"Oh, fuck, turn it down *turnitdown* -"

The veins leading down Sabina's arms and capillaries over her face suddenly rose to the surface, then - like grotesque flowers in bloom - exploded through her skin, one by one, spraying us, the room, her lifeless body with blood. It felt hot. I hadn't expected it to be hot. Or to notice the smell. Acrid iron hung in the air. The Vampire had unplugged the pump, but it continued to flow, adjusting to the reduced pressure in increments. The sac was half-full. My clothes were drenched. Her life ran down my face and past my tightly-closed lips. The Vampire was gawping at me, incandescent with rage.

"*Never*, in a year of doing this, have I been so fucking *reckless* -"

I walked out in a state of shock, leaving the Vampire

behind me. I took back alleys. I went to bed wearing the same clothes, my face brown and stiff. My brain had shut down.

Five

There's this old cliché that once you're covered in the blood of another person, you can never really wash it off. You'll find that the smell clings to you weeks later - flecks of brown in the creases between joints, in your ears, behind your eyelids every time you blink. The notion that no amount of washing will do any good.

The next morning, I woke up, threw my sheets into the disinfector and stepped into the shower. I was clean within minutes. I felt renewed. I called him right away.

We got past the anger fairly quickly. I promised I wouldn't just walk out again, even if things turned ugly. Within a fortnight, I was doing it by myself. Two blocks south, three blocks east, once a week. I wrote that first night in as a thrill-piece - the suggestion that a (non-existent) bystander had tipped off the watch, and in his haste the Vampire had botched the job. We received a sternly-worded correction letter from the deputy commissioner, which we printed at the back of the next day's edition in tiny, barely-legible script, but beyond that there were no repercussions. Apparently the Watch were just as intrigued by the mystery as the rest of our readership.

I was sat in a café with him after the first successful night, just as the sun broke over the horizon. He looked drained. When I sat down, he scrutinized me. He shrugged, shaking his head.

"What?" I asked.

"Nothing. I just... haven't met anyone like you before."

"Right. Cue thunderstorms and a swelling orchestra. You're old enough to be my Dad," I groaned. He rolled his eyes.

"Not like that. Just... don't confuse the fact that I'm methodical with some perverse sense of enjoyment. The first few weeks, I couldn't sleep. Even now, I get flashbacks. I was doing this to save my own skin - literally - but you're doing it to... what, chase a story?"

I looked down into my coffee. There was a dead ant floating in it, slowly swirling around clockwise. I pushed the mug away from me, and looked up at him.

"It's self-preservation. I've learned the hard way that you hold on to what you have, otherwise it can disappear from you in a heartbeat. I'll move on from this once I find another story that'll sustain me to the same degree, but in the meantime..." I shrugged.

"But... I mean, you get what we're doing, right? Killing people. Taking innocent lives."

I shook my head.

"No," I responded.

"This is bound to be good."

"Look. You need to understand this. You've probably been in some shitty places, I won't deny that, but when you finally die, you'll feel complete in the moment before your last breath. The moment your life starts to veer off the tracks, unless it's a controlled deviation, there are voices in the darkness, pushing you back. We live in a city where terror and death are just part of the fabric of society. You kill, it's because you're supposed to."

He looked at me, incredulous.

"You - you think what I did had a *point?* I did what I had

to because I wanted to *survive*, not to - what - find inner peace, is that what you think?"

"Don't think so short-term. You did what you did because you were told to, and the people who gave you your orders likely had their own. You were a pawn, protecting a king."

"Right. And?"

"And even the king's meaningless by itself. A chess board needs players to make sense."

He took a sip of his coffee, wincing at the heat. The sun streamed in through the windows. A couple, giggling and visibly drunk, stumbled in and ordered breakfast. The Vampire gazed at me.

"So... what does that make you? Another pawn? A player?"

"I...." The ant had stuck to the side of the mug. I drank, the hot liquid scalding the roof of my mouth, without blinking. "I don't think I'm anywhere near the board. I think - I think they forgot about me. Maybe I'm doing this to see if it makes enough noise to get me back in the game."

Six

Five knocks. My back ached. The camera blinked into life, and after a few seconds, the same gruff voice.

"Type?"

"O-negative. Five liters," I grunted.

"Send it up."

The hatch slid open, and I hauled the pouch off my shoulders and into the compartment. It closed, and there was a distant rumble. Electronic thunder. This part made me the most nervous - waiting around for payment. Not that the money was important, but standing around in an alley with no apparent purpose could easily draw attention. After a minute of softly hopping from one foot to the other, my headset updated with another 1,500.

"Next week?" came the voice from behind the camera.

"Sure. Probably."

"See you then."

"Can't say the same."

*

The next morning, bad news. Phil called me into his office.

"I know what you're going to offer, and I want you to pull it. Story's stale," he declared, shifting in his seat. I tried to keep my surprise as lacking in theatricality as possible.

"Stale? Someone died last night, Phil. I wouldn't call that stale," I said. He sighed.

"Yes, Erica, but someone's been dying in the same way once a week for the last three months. By this point, it's not something people want to read anymore. Any crime that carries on with the same regularity, regardless of how scary it is, people lose interest. It's like... cancer."

I gritted my teeth.

"*How* is it like cancer, Phil?"

"Look, Erica, don't get angry. My point is that about two or three people die of cancer every week, but it's hardly front-page news because it just *happens*. Do you have any leads on this? Any idea who did it? Basically, can we develop this at all?"

I paused, then my shoulders slumped.

"No."

"Then find something else. You're paid up for the rest of the week, anyway. Get back out there."

So I got out. The metro was quiet on weekday afternoons. Sitting there, watching buildings rush by, I felt out of the loop. I didn't know why I was going home first. I scanned through the information I'd stored on my specs, but the most recent was over a month old. I hadn't been keeping up. I didn't have a backup story. I'd expected this one to run for another few weeks.

Start simple, I guess. I opened up my contacts and dialed anyone I could.

"... Erica?"

Mark's voice, high-pitched but with the sort of confidence gleaned from too many lucky breaks, came through my specs. I still wasn't used to neural calls. They always felt invasive.

"Hi, Mark. I'm dry. You got anything?"

"Not like you, this. Thought you were usually in the loop?"

"I've been, uh, busy," I said, trying to keep the evasiveness from my voice.

"Oh? Sounds scandalous," he grinned.

"You don't know the half of it. So - got anything?"

"Bit of a dull week, I'm afraid. There's a biggie I'm working on, but you know how it is - can't really share details for that one," he said. I rolled my eyes. "Don't suppose you're interested in covering exam results?"

"What university?"

"Oh - no - it's a technical school, up in the suburbs. Construction skills, that sort of thing. Our best and brightest." I could hear him smirking through the static. Still, I didn't have much.

"Chance of inclusion in the edition?" I grumbled.

"Eh - I'd say about twenty percent. You know Phil doesn't go for feel-good stories unless there's some drama involved. It'd be less if we weren't running out of ideas. If you want better odds, find something yourself. You could always burn down the school, I suppose," he said, humorlessly. I clucked my tongue, thinking.

"Pass over the details. I'll use it if I don't find something better."

I started calling my other contacts, but all of them were either automatic disconnects - people in jail, or dead, or avoiding people like me - or didn't have anything. The air was muggy, warm, and just moving through it made me feel sluggish. Maybe on days like this, no-one could be bothered stirring up trouble. In a last-ditch effort, I called Tim.

"Tim. Give me something. There is *nothing* happening today." Silence on the other end. Then -

"Erica?" He sounded concerned.

"Yeah. Hi."

"I... I'm not sure I can help you."

"Right. Funny. Seriously - even armed robbery, minor assault, that sort of thing. You wouldn't *believe* the day I'm having."

"Look - tell me what you were doing in the Nixon Building this time last month. I know you don't live anywhere near there." I froze. "We have you on camera," he said, almost apologetically.

"... we?" It was all I could get out.

"Okay, I. As soon as I recognized you I requisitioned the data. But this could land me in *serious* hot water if it turns out that you - well, even if you're not implicated, you know what happened there. You wrote it, after all. *And* lied about our response. Thanks for that, by the way," he scolded.

I tried to sound even. Even so, my voice was a little shaky.

"Are you... *implying* something, Tim?"

He sighed.

"I don't know, Erica. Am I? All I know is that if I help you from now on, it's not because you have something over me. You know how I got this job - and, honestly, I'm starting to wonder *how* you know - but I have evidence that puts you as a potential person of interest. I'd say that makes us even."

I hung up.

I was at a loss.

I had nothing.

I called the one person who I knew would pick up.

Seven

The same café. No ants this time, but there was a squashed roach on the floor near our table. I wasn't sure why we'd come back here, other than familiarity. The Vampire sat across from me. He looked... healthier. The beginnings of a tan, and his hands - previously wrinkled, thick stubby fingers with the nails bitten off savagely - looked healthier. A pianist's hands, rather than those of a killer. He smiled when I walked in.

"I was wondering when I'd see you again. You look... worried. This line of work finally getting to you?" I shook my head, in a way that I hoped said "shut the fuck up". He seemed to get the message. Even so, when he dipped his head, he looked like a wounded deer. I felt the faintest pang of guilt. When it became clear that I wasn't going to say anything, he spoke again. Timidly, this time. "So... what's up?"

And I told him. Everything, from our circulation figures, to the thrill of adrenaline when I saw my credits rising, and then back to my first day on the job as a journalist, how I'd walked in with a drive full of my collated notes and watched as, one by one, the jaws of everyone in the building dropped to the floor. How I'd left those notes by the wayside in the pursuit of this - a story that I honestly, desperately thought was the Big One. How the way that this sort of thing worked was as an unbroken thread - cut things off, and finding the heartbeat of the city was nearly impossible.

"How'd you find it to begin with?" he asked.

I'd been thinking the same thing myself. I tried to cast my mind back. Eighteen-year-old me. That initial, blinding sense of opportunity. Maybe it was the fact that I was at the bottom myself - so many of those links to so-called "criminals" came naturally because, in a sense, I was one. I was only mistrusted in the sense that I was new, not because I had to break down income barriers or figure out the right way to talk to gang members. Now, with my comfortable apartment and comfortable salary and comfortable life, I wouldn't know where to start. When you start to rise, your old links start to feel less like they're earned and more like blind luck. He nodded while I told him this. I had a feeling he knew a little too well what I was talking about. Again, I found myself wondering what he had done to have to pay his debts in such a macabre way.

"I'm lost. I really... don't know where to go next. My one lead is a technical school a couple of miles from here. Dullest fucking story of the century."

"Break-in?"

"Exam results day," I said, wincing.

He laughed. I looked at him, hopefully. He had been confident before, but in the past it had come with an edge. Now, he seemed totally at peace.

"So... do you think you can help?" He started, looking

thrown.

"I... I mean, I haven't heard from anyone in weeks. I told you - when you found me, that was my last week. I'm free - time to make something of myself, you know?" It struck me that behind his ludicrous moniker, behind a hackneyed mythos, I knew nothing about this man. "But... damn, I dunno." He paused. "No luck in... whatever it was you were trying to do? How's everything looking besides work?" I shook my head.

"There *is* nothing besides work."

"Maybe you're supposed to feel this so the pay-off later on holds more weight. If you think about it, chess pieces don't actually know they're in play. Just knowing about CAIN is weird enough," he leveled.

I smirked.

"Sure. Very optimistic of you."

We sat in silence for a moment. I tried to change the subject.

"What have you been doing since... you know?" I asked.

"Just sitting around, mostly. Like, honestly, I'm glad that I don't have to kill people anymore, but I'm not sure what I *should* be doing. Most of my friends were locked up while I was off on my, uh..."

"... sabbatical," I ventured. He grinned.

"Sure." He sighed, and took a sip from his drink. "You'd think prison wouldn't exist in a world like this. Maybe some people need it." He sighed. "If you're used to being a criminal, I guess it gets you away from the pressures of the real world."

His eyes shimmered for a second, and he breathed in sharply - then the look vanished, and he exhaled slowly.

"So that's what it meant. Ha!" He laughed mirthlessly,

staring into his coffee.

"What?"

"Nothing. Just an idea. I... I've just realized I may have something for you. Didn't make any sense before today, but... I think this might actually end well for both of us."

"Oh?" I remarked, confused.

"Give me a couple of days to iron things out. You okay until then?" he asked. I nodded. His whole demeanor had shifted, and I wasn't sure why.

Eight

It was forty-eight hours to the minute later when he sent me the message.

Briar Estate, Building A. 2am. Seventh floor. Make sure you install a magnifier on your specs.

That was it. No mention of what I would find there. I slid my knife into my jacket pocket. Something seemed strange, but I couldn't quite place it until I arrived in the dead of night. It took me an hour to walk there, letting the sound of the city fade away, seeing the streetlights grow ever sparser. This didn't feel like dangerous territory, though. The people I saw just decreased in number, rather than appearing more threatening. There were overgrown fields, here. Former farmland. Even debris, left behind from hundreds of years ago. There was the feeling that the whole district had only recently been brought inside the wall.

The Briar Estate complex was a construction site. I could hear the wind rushing around the concrete pillars. A security barrier had recently been disabled, and it swung open at the slightest touch. It was dark - not dark in the sense of a back alley downtown, but dark in the sense of only being lit by the moon. The whole place felt like a graveyard.

I climbed up the temporary stairwell to the seventh floor. There, the wind was even louder, rushing against my ears, turning the tips of my fingers numb. I made my way to the east side, slowly feeling my way through the darkness, terrified in the knowledge that a step to my left and I would be sent plummeting to the ground. About halfway across, I saw something taped to the ground. I crouched, and squinted through the darkness.

And gasped.

There was his photo, and next to it... his name. And date of birth, and home address, and employment records for the last twenty years. Family history. A full biography. I felt like I'd been punched in the chest. Still reeling, the next message caught me off guard.

Straight ahead. I'm in Building B.

I lifted my head gingerly, as if losing eye contact might allow the information to disappear, and then everything clicked into place.

From this distance, he looked... *so* vulnerable. His hands - those delicate, pianist's fingers - were behind his head, and he was kneeling, looking out at me. A light powered by a portable generator was illuminating him from behind, and it was hard to tell, but he looked like he was smiling.

I had no idea what to do. Part of me knew what was going on, but refused to put the pieces together. I had come out expecting a drug deal, or corporate fraud, or something sensational but safe. Not this. Not him. I closed my eyes and sent over a message.

Why?

For a moment, he scratched his cheek, then replaced his hand behind his head. For a long time, he knelt there, looking pensive. He closed his eyes, and as a dozen police officers in riot gear rushed upstairs and surrounded him, he smiled. They cuffed him. I could make out Tim in the background, looking smug. The Vampire opened his eyes, looking directly at me. He knew that I had an exclusive. Story of the fucking century.

I guess you're back on the board.

THE RESERVE

...

How did I get here?

Right. Yes. Another fall. Those hips aren't what they used to be. I remember *that*, but not how I got here. How did I - no, I just asked that.

I recognize her. Andrea. No. Ruby. Ruby is the virtual interface designed to check my vitals. Drab. No personality. Andrea is... I... how did I get here?

Chapter One

"What sort of name is Andrea?"

"One you like. As I already explained, my form and vocal presentation are perfectly designed for your comfort and full understanding. I have determined that "Andrea" is a name that inspires within you a feeling of security and an open mind."

She's about 1.6m tall, a little shorter than me, but has a commanding presence about her. It's once I get out of my cot and put my hand right through her, only noticing afterwards the tiny holographic projector embedded in the wall, that I put two and two together. Still - it doesn't get rid of the immediate thoughts I have upon seeing her. Her hair is spiked into an indigo mohawk. She's wearing a tight-fitting leather jacket, black bikini bottoms, and spike-tipped boots that make me weak at the knees. All of it not real, but some parts of my body hadn't noticed. I was more than a little confused.

"So. Um. Andrea. Anything I can do for you?"

"I've come to give you advice for when you come to the surface. You have a couple of months until the pod shutters open - it's only fair that you're given some time to prepare."

"Advice?"

"Yes. CAIN is not a prescriptive entity, Alex. We do not give orders. There are harsh punishments for those who stray so far from its design that they irreparably endanger the paths of others, but for most transgressions we have contingency plans built in."

"I thought you said you were designed for my understanding? None of that made sense."

"My advice is for your benefit. I strongly suggest you take it, but no-one's going to force you. We just won't necessarily be there to catch you if you don't take it and then fuck up. Basically, I'm not your mother."

I smile. This attitude suits her better.

"I... had no illusions on that front." Her breasts rise and fall. She looks annoyed. I'm torn between imagining kissing her and the thought of her slamming me against the wall and grinding against me. Neither of them are possible, of course. That doesn't exactly help. "So. Uh. What should I do?"

"Do you like the idea of fucking for money?"

My body immediately responds, but it takes a moment to open my mouth.

"Um. You mean -"

"I mean you hand-pick your clients. You have full security at your disposal. No agency in control, but all the benefits of one. We've got suggested starting rates for various services rendered that we guarantee will get you repeat business." She gestures to the blank space next to her, which dissolves to reveal a slide with a dizzying array of numbers. Big numbers. "Based on the breadth of your preferences and tastes, I'm going to call it and say that about 85% of your job will contain a fair amount of intrinsic satisfaction."

I laugh.

"Calling me easy, Andrea?"

She fixes me with a cool gaze.

"Yes."

I cough nervously.

"The remaining 15% you can either choose to forgo, at a minor cost to your extrinsic quality of life, or take for the money. I'm estimating that you'll probably take it." She pauses for a moment, allowing it all to sink in. "Honestly, the most negative experience we foresee happening is boredom. Based on your viewing history and flick preferences, you don't appear to be disgusted by anything." Immediately, I flash back to two nights ago: *Snow White and the Seven Dildo-Wielding Amputees*. It's still sitting there in my collection. I resolve to delete it as soon as she leaves. All that said, everything so far has been terrifyingly on point.

"Anything else? You seem to know a lot about me."

"I know everything about you, Alex. You should know that as a holographic construct, *I* can't pleasure you in any way. There's plenty of that on the surface, though." I turn bright red. "You'll find that the fact that you get flustered at statements like that works in your favor, too. You'd be surprised at what people are into."

"Wh-" I gather myself. "What about where I live? Is there anyone I should be meeting about that?"

Andrea nods. We're back to businesslike. Thank fuck.

"We've set you up in an apartment in the center of the leisure district. Full soundproofing, though that's mostly for the sake of your clients - you'll have an adjunct room where you work when clients don't call you out to their own homes. You'll find it fully-stocked with everything you might need for six months when you arrive, but after that you'll be required to fend for yourself. I'm going to assume you're resourceful enough for that. You seem like a good boy." She smirks. I feel like I'm being toyed with, and I really don't mind.

She straightens up. "Two months. I recommend you get to grips with the layout of the city - you'll find a full map and virtual tour in your specs. I'm also providing you with the contact details of a few clubs and bars in the area once you start looking for work - they'll provide you with a steady stream of clients. Good luck, cutie." She smiles, and dissolves away, leaving the room empty. It takes the rest of the evening for the aching between my legs to fade away.

*

I groan. Ruby isn't due back for another hour, and I desperately need to urinate. I grab the handrail next to the bed, and push myself up. Don't have to do this often. My bones feel like they could crack at any moment.

Little by little, I inch along. Better this indignity than having someone discover me and suffer the embarrassment of being cleaned up. Finally, positioned over the bowl, legs apart, I grab the rails on either side and dangle uselessly, surrendering control to my bladder. The door to the bathroom is locked. There is some small solace in the knowledge that no-one has to see this.

Chapter Two

"Come in, boy."

Edward Tinderbox stands by the window, framed in neon light, one arm leaning against a marble pillar and the other idly holding a martini glass. To call his office opulent would be an understatement - as I step in, I can hear the throbbing industrial electronica from downstairs, but even the bass thump is silenced once the door closes. Everything is gold-edged. A panther snarls at me from a cage in the corner. There are two men on each side of the door, both of whom feel like subjects of real-life image manipulation - drag to resize, and you end up with these hulking beasts.

Edward, on the other hand, is adorned with a coat saturated with a million microscopic LED lights, arranged today to give the effect of waves breaking against an ocean he'll never see. It's mesmerizing to watch. His head bobs above the coat, almost as if disembodied. He turns around slowly. Black kohl eyeliner has been applied with surgical precision - presumably by someone else. And there's the infamous neck tattoo - QUEEN BITCH in flaming green letters, equal parts gaudy and intimidating.

Edward is not a man to be fucked with. Even I know that.

I sit down. He shakes his head. I stand up. He beckons me toward the window. We stare out across as the leisure district, a monument to excess, decked out in lights as dazzling as the desert sun. When he next speaks, it's barely audible.

"Did you ever wonder why I never asked for your services personally, Alex?"

The question surprises me. Only a handful of club proprietors have asked to sample the goods before they assign me clients. I can list them off fairly quickly. Mr. Samsa, proprietor of the Blue Cat Jazz Café. He lay there silently, soundless even at the point of climax, and had tears of joy in his eyes and couldn't stop thanking me afterwards. Ursula Phoenix, the owner of hardCANDI, who bent me over and took me from behind, left red welts on my ass and bruises on my chest, and tied my genitals up so tightly that I couldn't walk straight for a week. And Indigo - oh, Indigo - who asked to spend twelve hours with me, then denied me access to any of her clientele but promised me a huge recurring fee if I came back to her place once a month. The rest had been strictly professional. Either way suited me. All this said, Edward had asked a leading question. I decided to go along with it.

"Once or twice, yes. I put it down to trust."

"Do not confuse trust with disinterest, Alex. More than one complaint, and I would see to it that you'd never work again."

"Sorry, Edward, but I don't think you have that power." As soon as I say it, I regret it. Thankfully, after a beat, he cracks a smile, tilts his head, and shrugs. A maybe-you're-right shrug. I wonder how many individuals have been executed on the spot for lesser statements. I think about the distribution of power. How the man beside me, who emerged on the surface eight years ago and cultivated an entertainment empire, is only half a rung up from me when it comes to invulnerability. The thought relaxes me a little.

He sighs, and looks down at the dancefloor. Even from this vantage point, you can see the sweat pouring down their necks, work out the beat from the way that people are grinding against each other. A girl who looks like she's just appeared on the surface grins, slides her hands down the pants of a man easily ten years her senior, and drags him off to a darkened corner with deviant intent.

"What do you think? We actually pipe sex pheromones in to a limited degree. Just enough to let them think they're in control."

I grin, and head back to my seat as he gestures me over. We sit. He pours us both a drink.

"Lucrative."

He groans. "*Meaningless.* To me, anyway. I created this carnival of lust because I am *fascinated* by the inaccessible, boy. I see a tanned, perfectly-defined man like you and it's like looking at a painting - intriguing, but utterly devoid of eroticism. Likewise, that nubile young girl I spotted you eyeing up. Of course some part of me understands that she's beautiful, but I just don't... *care*, you know? Sex interests me in a purely academic sense." He laughs, his voice flecked with distant frost. "You're a brilliant case study in that respect, boy. I could watch you work all day, and never get bored, but I feel about as seduced by your presence as I would by a brick wall."

I sigh, and sip from my drink, trying to avoid gagging - martinis never agree with me. I try and keep things professional. Edward is known for long, introspective monologues, and unless he's paying me to listen I'm not interested. Nothing personal. That's kind of the point.

"So... what? You brought me here to study me?" He's lost in his drink. Finally, he sits up straight and fixes me with a cool glare.

"No. I have an offer, of sorts."

"Go on."

"You've heard of Steven K. Petersen, I assume? Just opened a new club in the Northern outskirts. All class and no character. Think he's called the place the Hairy Haddock, or something equally revolting."

"Scarlet Sturgeon. I wondered about that name too." He rolls his eyes.

"Honestly. Anyway, I want you to refuse any offers of business. I want his club closed within the month, and if I can deny him the reputation that comes with a man like you, then I'm going to do it."

I stare at my fingernails. They're in dire need of a trim. I always let them grow out a little - some clients like being scratched.

"What's in it for me?"

"I pay you a weekly stipend."

"How much?"

"Five thousand." I snort. I know he wants me to haggle, but that's an absurd start. "Okay, fine, ten." I shake my head. "Twenty? Even you have to set limits on your time available, Alex."

"No. Won't do it."

I can see him turn red beneath his makeup.

"Are you *refusing* me?"

I sigh, exasperated.

"Yes. It's not just the money, Edward. I don't mean to offend you, but Mikael's clients are actually *interesting*.

And, for the most part, take care of themselves. Every time I come here, I'm still cleaning off the spray tan the next morning." He raises his hand.

"Do you realize that I could have you killed right here?"

I roll my eyes. Maybe part of me is intimidated, but it's a purely instinctive reaction. Snipers have been trained on all of us since I arrived, and he knows it.

"You wouldn't be the first to try. Besides, you're smart. I bring in a shitload of money for you. I still will, even if Mikael ends up as big as you. Like I said, his clients are already different to yours. Different ponds."

He looks at the two men by the door, then away, thinking. Finally, after a few beats, he relaxes, looking downcast.

"Fine. I just... I really don't like that guy, Alex. Promise me you won't leave me for him?" All of a sudden, this mogul looks very pathetic. I walk over, bend down, and put my arms around him.

"Never. Even I need thick-headed predictability as part of my schedule. And besides - despite your threats, you're too fun." He smiles guiltily, and I kiss the cheek he offers to me. In the space of a minute, he's returned to his normal self. Behind me, I hear the guards relax, and the faintest sound of relieved exhalation.

Downstairs, in the dark, the man I spotted earlier is on his knees, his mouth full. I raise my eyebrows at the girl, who looks me up and down with a dead look in her eyes, and blinks out a transfer of two thousand to me. There's very little I won't do for two thousand. As it happens, there's very little I end up doing. Boring as they are, Edward's clients usually have more money than sense. Hard to give something like that up.

The only other thing I get out of that night is a nickname

that spreads like wildfire. Long Tongue Silver. Compared to some of the horrors I've heard, I feel like I'm getting off lightly.

*

I still have nightmares about the dark. Even here, when the lights are always on and there's usually someone on the corridor groaning or yelling. Never a moment's peace when you're packed in like sardines. But still. There are nights when I close my eyes, and finally get comfortable, and within minutes I'm covered in the same cold sweat. The day-to-day makes no sense anymore, but some parts of the past are etched on my memory.

Chapter Three

They arrive in the night.

There's a blinding flash, then paralysis and darkness. The feeling of cold hands against my skin, lifting my frozen body. A low rumble. Stinging pinpricks on every inch of my body. And then -

"Hello, stranger."

My eyes snap open, and there she is, luminescent against a grey backdrop. The whole room feels clammy, but she radiates warmth.

"You."

I try moving. No luck. In my peripheral vision, I can see wires, rust, and electrodes on my body. Cold air on the back of my head, but otherwise numb. Too exposed. The only thing I can really control is my mouth, and even that feels numb.

"Best if you don't try, dear. The paralytic's supposed to stay active for another twelve hours, but there's no reason to test it. And, uh, you don't want to mess around with the stuff they're doing back there. I take it you remember me?"

I close my eyes, and open them. She's still there.

"Of course. Andrea. Been a while. Didn't think I'd be seeing you again."

"Me neither."

There's an odd tension in the room. Maybe I'm just imagining it.

"What am I doing here?" She sighs.

"Now *there's* a question." She flickers briefly. "Let's start with the basics. You know about CAIN?" The name sounds familiar. I concentrate.

"That's what the higher-ups call the Strategy, right? What keeps us ticking along, or whatever?"

"The Central Artificial Intelligence Network, yes. It's where I was produced. It's the hub designed to extrapolate new information about human behavior, desires and motivations from the two hundred years of research conducted after you retreated underground. Its core goal was to create meaningful lives, minimizing conflict and carefully balancing the interplay between each individual. I should have known you wouldn't have done your homework."

"Was?"

"Uhuh. It's currently offline. I'm just a crude archive copy they pulled. In fact, the closest I get to any agency of my own is the ability to tell you that my higher functions are currently incapacitated. The Andrea you saw as a kid was fully capable of complex thought and free agency. I'm little more than a mouthpiece."

I notice the walls again. Unfamiliar. This is room I was never supposed to see. This all feels haphazard, and the pieces are starting to fall into place. Over in the corner, a faded poster flakes off the wall. *TWO HUNDRED YEARS OF RESEARCH FOR A BETTER FUTURE, GUIDED BY A CENTRAL ARTIFICIAL INTELLIGENCE NETWORK*. It looks ancient. Out of the corner of my eye, I can spot moss on the ground, inching through the cracks in the cement.

"If it's so crucial, why is it offline?"

"Because CAIN got too efficient. Its primary goal was to create *meaningful* life - not long, not prosperous, but life that felt complete at its end. It had to be able to create the conditions for ending lives, otherwise nothing would work - you can't have a meaningful life that just trails off. And yes, there were some soft limits in place - a general promotion of health, and the desire to extend life to reasonable ends, but... well, maybe they were a little too soft." I breathe in. "So the first generation of children on the surface is born, and suddenly we notice that they start dying. Freak accidents, exposure to diseases they would never usually encounter - it was all oblique enough that tracing it was extraordinarily difficult, but you need to understand something, Alex. If there was a trend in the way that people live and die, CAIN was *always* responsible."

I close my eyes for five, six, seven seconds. This is all a lot to take in, and I still don't know why *me* - why am I being told this?

"Those overseeing CAIN had the sense to figure out that the high probability for a tidy conclusion with infant death - no great issues to resolve, no catharsis to achieve, just a simple existence to resolve within a year or two - was so powerful that it was overriding everything else, even those soft limits. It was something they hadn't foreseen. And, worse still, because CAIN was designed to predict events like this long before they occurred, they have no idea where to set a restore point. So... they fell back on contingency planning." With those last words, she looks directly at me. Or through me. I'm not sure.

"Contingency?"

She smiles.

"Rather than using CAIN to advise pod residents two months before their eighteenth birthday, two human agents will be sent to seed those goals and aspirations when each turns eleven. They'll have a full range of sedatives and relaxants at their disposal, as well as psychotropic drugs if need be - whatever gets the job done. When this was planned, it was already accepted that humans could never match the nuance of CAIN." She sounds smug when she says this. It's easy to forget that she's just another part of the machine. "Those two agents would together be assigned to one pod, and track the five individuals through their lives, carrying out a... blunter version of CAIN's capabilities. Square one. They'd be carrying out the programming of a computer with colossal banks of information, and excellent powers of deduction, but with no imaginative capacity. Just enough to keep things ticking over until they wake her up."

"When will that be?"

She shrugs.

"At least ten years. Maybe twenty. There were billions of restore points, Alex, and there are currently no obvious indicators of where the overseers should focus. They'll eventually narrow it down, but it's going to take time."

The next part, I can already feel coming.

"So - you'll be partnered with someone. You already have a pod assigned, and -"

"Wait!" I splutter, spit flecking down my chin. It feels

cold. "I have... *no* idea what to do."

"Oh. Of course. You'll get full training in a few seconds. In fact, just about... now."

I black out. Colors swim in front of me. Every nerve, tendon and organ feels warped out of shape. Pain engulfs me. When I wake up minutes, hours, weeks later, I know everything. I have an emotional history with a partner I've never met. I already know that when we first encounter each other, everything will already feel routine, just with an edge.

I breathe heavily.

"I know kung fu," I say, though I'm not sure why. An echo of something I watched as a kid.

"Good luck," Andrea says, the room darkens, and I wake up in my bed, renewed.

*

It took a lot longer than twenty years.

Someone who looks solid walks into the room. He looks young. He peers down at me.

"Alex? How are you feeling today?"

Ruby dissolves into view.

"Mr. Teuthan currently suffers from facial muscular atrophy, which renders him unable to speak approximately 95% of the time."

Ruby's real job is to remind other, fitter people how useless my body is. Yes, her presence keeps me alive, but at some human cost.

The intern - intern? He looks like an intern - nods, and walks out, looking awkward. Off to find someone else to gawp at.

The truth is that today, if I put my mind to it, I could muster a few words - but I don't want to. My head is in the past. On improbable pairings, and the impossibility of molding a life, and how knowledge and expertise are nothing without experience. The way those kids grew up.

Chapter Four

"Last one. You remember the details?"

"Yep. No sedation, begin with no introduction, get to the point with minimal interruptions. I read the brief. She seems like a real charmer."

Rachida glares at me. After today, we'll only meet once a year until the first resident climbs onto the surface, and things are still chilly between us. Part of me puts it down to difference of outlook - whoever paired a schoolteacher with a sex worker at least had a sense of humor. Or maybe teaching was really her calling. Either way, I can tell by the atmosphere around her that she's counting down the seconds until we break for the interim.

"What if she acts surprised? Or if she panics?" Rachida asks, her brow furrowed.

"She won't," I murmur.

"Actually, there's a 5.3% chance that she will."

"Then we fall back to the usual. Masks on, restrain her until the gas kicks in."

"You're far too laid back," she says. "These are people we're dealing with, here. They could do anything."

"Sorry, weren't you the one just discussing probability ratios?"

If looks could kill, the effects of the nuclear blast created by the glare she shoots in my direction would probably wipe out civilization for good. Sometimes, I wonder if I'm not deliberately winding her up to see if she'll crack.

I bring up the time on my specs. Eight minutes.

"You studied this kid much?" She murmurs noncommittally. "She's an odd one. Really methodical. Spends most of her time reading, never goes out. Kind of makes you a bit concerned."

"We're making her a killer. That doesn't concern you?"

I shake my head.

"Nah. You saw the rationale. It kind of makes sense. I mean, would you rather be assassinated in the prime of your life or wither away on a hospital bed?"

"Wither away."

"Really?" She looks deadly serious. "Why?"

"Just dying when it feels appropriate is selfish."

"... huh."

We stand there for the last few minutes in silence. The door opens. It always shocks me how young they look. It strikes me that this is the first time I've ever seen this girl in the flesh. This is one of the five people for whom I have to act as some strange guardian angel, and she's already fully-formed. That feeling, along with the probing, curious yet calm look she's giving me, already sets me on edge.

"Ordinarily, we'd be feeding gas into your room and insinuating this into your unconscious memory, but I can already tell that's not going to wash with you."

Chapter Five

Older, now. We are sitting in a surveillance room a couple of blocks away from a tower where one of our charges has brutally murdered Sabina Hasan, a petty thief and addict who on average left her house once every two months. No great loss, but it's still grotesque just to sit and watch. Even after everything else.

"What is it?" Rachida looks concerned. "You know we can't do anything."

"I know."

When you keep such close tabs on people - when you can track their neural processes and predict every single move they make - you witness the sort of darkness that would otherwise fade into an undercurrent. A gun in someone's mouth is obvious from the outside, but we have to be able to see that same gun in the mind's eye of all five. Every ugly impulse, no matter how small, is marked down. Every good one, too, but somehow they don't stick in your head as much.

Erica is shakily getting to her feet, her partner gesturing angrily at her. We track her leaving the building.

"Intentions?"

"Just going home, by the looks of it. We can probably punch out for the night, as long as this little clusterfuck's tied up. You got a link to the other guy's overseer?"

"Sure."

A face obscured by darkness flashes up. For all we know, they might be sitting meters away from us, separated by a couple of soundproof walls.

"Yes?" The voice pipes through, the pitch altered, the cadence skewed away from anything remotely human.

"Calling in a risk assessment. We need to requisition the intentions of your man in the Nixon building." There's a pause.

"Sent. Don't think you have anything to worry about. He's pretty methodical. No extra clean-up necessary. Fine to release to the Watch in an hour or so. Long-term, he's planning to turn himself in. Should be nice and tidy."

"Cheers." He fades back into the dark.

I scan over the results. A few flares of anger around the edges, but aside from that he has every base covered. I exhale.

"I need a fucking drink," Rachida sighs. I'm startled. This is out of character. "You coming?"

Once the shock subsides, I grab my coat and we step out into the night.

A few hours and a few pints later, she surprises me again. And again. We all channel our frustration into different pursuits, I suppose. Afterwards, she curls up next to me, a sheen of sweat glinting off her exposed shoulder.

"Let's keep this simple, okay," she slurs. I laugh. "No, seriously." She straightens up, and concentrates intently on a speck of non-existent dirt under a fingernail. "I have... a few reasons why I don't want a relationship. Not right now. It doesn't really go well with this line of work." She looks troubled. I don't want to pry. I put up my hands.

"That's fine. Sometimes, I think you forget about my old job." She smirks.

"Right. Mm. Long Tongue Silver."

"So... we're good?" She eases back down, her head on my chest, her eyes closed.

"We're good," she murmurs, and falls asleep.

*

Another intern - or maybe she's a nurse, I don't know - is swimming in front of my field of vision. She's talking slowly, and I catch the words "let me know if you need", but other than that it's like trying to communicate across an ocean with a couple of tin cans and a piece of string. Black inkblots stain my periphery. Once she leaves, and the silence returns, I start to notice my own breathing.

It's shallower than it was. More ragged.

Maybe this is it.

Chapter Six

We meet three years earlier, for the first time since the inductions, out on the fringes of the city. Today, surveillance is in an upstairs panic room of a house that was abandoned hundreds of years ago. Rachida has been arranging an order for farming equipment to Geraldo's new home; I've been tracking his movements since he stepped onto the surface. So far, so predictable.

The girl behind the shop counter has freckles and the sort of enthusiastic disposition that could get wearing after, say, an hour. When Geraldo steps in, she bounds up to him, all smiles, and he looks a little taken aback. Poor kid.

Rachida sits down next to me and adjusts her specs.

"Did I miss anything?"

"Nope. Kid's mostly been wandering around, looking dazed. Mostly heading in the right direction, though, so I'm not worried. You? Any issues with the manufacturer?"

"Apart from a few questions, no. You'd think they'd learn to stay ignorant."

"Charming."

We sit there in silence for a few moments. The girl is back at the counter, and lights up when Geraldo walks over with a bottle in his hand. He laughs when she says he's the only person she's seen today. Leans against the counter. One of the background graphs spikes, and Rachida leans in.

"Well, hello...." She blinks, and the offending chart in question slides into the foreground. "Looks like someone's getting a little excited. What do you think?"

I run a few calculations.

"Nothing to write home about. Both of them are

basically paragons of hard work and blissfully dull stability. They'll get along just fine."

Geraldo is murmuring, now. He seems more at ease. Then he says something, and Rachida gasps.

"Well, *that's* forward. Fuck," I laugh. "Let me rewind that. I want to be sure I heard it right." There it is. Seven words we didn't quite expect from someone whose ideal lifestyle involves mucking out stables. We snap back. The girl's grabbed his arm, and they're in the shop's office. She's pinned against the wall, moaning, and he has one hand on the back of her head as he kisses her hard and slides his hand down the front of her jeans. Part of me feels proud for this kid, in some perverse way.

Rachida doesn't look impressed.

"Oh, come on," I exclaim, gesturing at the action on screen, "it's sweet! Look how sweet it i- oh, wow...." The faint, rhythmic sound of skin on skin slips into our ears. Rachida is shaking her head, exasperated. They finish, stunningly quickly. Both look satisfied. I sigh. "What I wouldn't give to have my eighteen-year-old body back. I miss getting erections on demand."

"Pig."

"Oh, come on. You have to admit it's kind of adorable. Not everyone gets that sort of meet-cute."

"I have to work with you for how long, exactly?"

I wilt a little. She softens.

"Sorry. I just - I know that we had time to prepare and everything, but I didn't really want to leave teaching. I know I got a good seven years out of it, but... I don't know. I'm going to miss it. It's not your fault."

"It's okay." And it is. "I'll try to be less, um...."

"Blunt?" I frown.

"Sure."

"Good."

We sit back, and silently watch them clean up.

Chapter Seven

We're in full-on damage control mode. Rachida is in conference calls all day, liaising with other overseers to establish an acceptable cover for any concerned parties, and I've been tweaking algorithms and constructing the scene of an only-slightly implausible mysterious disappearance with the overseer of Mikael Simms. So far, it's been tough. Simms was high-profile.

"So - tell me again what happened." Even past the vocal masking, you can hear the desperation in this guy's voice.

"I just... lost track, you know? This guy isn't - wasn't - the only important client I had."

"Client?"

"Sure. What do you call them?"

"I don't. You were telling me how you fucked up so hard."

"I just... okay, so let's say hypothetically that in addition to this guy, you're also in charge of a crime boss who always seems to be pushing the limits in terms of what he can get away with, conjoined twins at a fetish club and one of the highest-grossing skin flick stars in the entire city. You know. Just a fucking hypothetical. Against that sort of backdrop, a few murders don't exactly stand out, you know? And, well. You know. I at least caught one of them."

"That first one? Sure. But only once it was noticed. You should have spoken to us then, you know."

"I didn't know he'd seen it, did I?"

148

"Whatever. I'm just glad our guy turned up at just the right time to provide a crucial part of the cover."

"What's the story there?"

"None of your fucking business," I snarl. "We're giving him the job Simms was doing, and that's all you need to know. As far as anyone's concerned, he was the one that uncovered the whole plot."

This is a really rough week. I've found myself masturbating whenever I'm in danger of dwelling too much on recent events, just to stop from thinking. I keep coming back to the look on Tim's face. It's starting to fade now, but he looked haunted for days. There's a reason we're confined to the shadows - even with the soft paternalism of CAIN, no-one likes the idea of their lives being subject to an architect's vision. Even though it had worked out for the best, Tim encountering us had been the least awful scenario we could come up with. It was that, or allow a rampage to continue unchecked. Or even let a man with three flags on his account be murdered, ensuring enough administrative bullshit to last for another decade. And this wasn't even our job.

I *hate* doing other people's jobs.

"So here's what I've got for you. Mikael was secretly harboring psychopathic tendencies, which he relieved by murdering innocents at night. Tim was on watch, received an anonymous tip-off, and it sparked his own independent investigation - the one that led to Mikael's exposure and summary termination. You want further details, it's in your file. I've given you full read access."

"Not write?"

"You're fucking hilarious."

"Mikael wasn't a psychopath."

"Mikael's dead. Asshole."

I close the link, pinching the bridge of my nose.

Tim will recover from this. All current estimates have him overcoming his little peek behind the curtain, and staying quiet about it as long as he has gainful employment - which we plan to ensure he keeps. He'll be okay. He gets to be the calm at the center of a swirling tornado of idiocy. Lucky him.

Rachida pokes her head in.

"How you doing in here?" I wince. My head is throbbing. "That bad, huh? I'm done on my end. If you want to take the rest of the night off, I can do the tracking for the next few hours. Looks like you could use some rest."

I get to my feet shakily. I've been sat in the same spot for about twelve hours, and my legs forget to function for a moment. I grimace a thank-you, and head for the door.

"Hey." I stop. I'm right next to her, both of us wedged in the doorframe. She smiles warmly, inexplicably - not the smile of someone who's endured a day of frantic planning. She rests a hand on my chest and kisses me. Her hand slowly wanders down between my legs, and despite everything we've endured today I can feel myself stiffen. Old habits die hard. She pulls back, and grins. "Go on, get some sleep."

*

You always had more energy than me when push came to shove. Even now, as you're sitting next to my bed, your eyes shining and your hand gripping mine, there's a flicker of envy when I think of how you'll go on living, unfaltering, upright and sharp until your last.

It's just a flicker, though.

Mostly, this feels right. Everything loses its staying power given enough time, even memories. A few more months, and I might not even remember you.

Ruby emerges to give the cold, clinical diagnosis, and you wave her away.

"I know."

Just a few more breaths. I don't have any more words, only expressions, but I know you can read them. You close your eyes, and a tear runs down your cheek, and you grip my hand a little tighter.

We never really dated. We fucked, and laughed at each other's stupid jokes, but also went through long periods of hostility, and businesslike functionality, and ultimately didn't suffer for it. We didn't have expectations. We just happened to spend a lot of time around each other, whether we liked it or not.

Still - it makes sense that you're here. Monitoring the lives of others teaches you that everything is transient. Cathartic moments and emotional threads are robbed from all of us at every turn. But you were constant. In a world full of chaos, you at least made sense.

Frozen in this perfectly still moment, nothing feels interrupted.

Chapter Eight

Rachida is gazing up at the bridge out of the city. We're a hundred meters below them, a couple of deckchairs set out, mobile monitors clicking away idly next to us. Rafi has been standing on the edge for about half an hour now. Rachida still can't get past the idea that people use virtual interface droids as sex aids.

"I just think it's a little gross. Honestly, even if the droid wasn't based on the likeness of his ex, it's still kind of weird."

"That's a little...."

"What?"

"I mean, there's a rainbow-striped strap-on dildo and a fursuit in your closet that render your judgments a little hypocritical."

"Shut up." She can't help but grin, though. "Even you have to admit that getting a VI based on a real person is unethical."

I half-nod, half-shrug. "Sure. But it's hard to draw the line with this sort of thing. It's hardly like he was taking her for walks." I sigh. "I try not to get into ethics, though. We've seen far worse. I'm not sure we're the best-equipped to address those sorts of concerns."

Rachida dips her head.

"Remind me why we're here?" I ask. "Shouldn't we be trying to prevent him from jumping?"

"Nope," she replies. "You're witnessing something very special, here. A perfect balance of outcomes."

"And by that you mean...."

"If he jumps, it's a tragic end, but given his sordid past it still brings with it a sense of narrative closure. Self-sacrifice for the sake of never hurting anyone again, if that makes sense." She sighs. "If he steps down, though...."

"... he keeps hurting people?" I ask, confused.

"Indicators point to no, at the moment. Looks like our man is having an epiphany of sorts up there. The murderer-turned-peace-activist kind. If he steps down, it'll likely stick."

"*If* he steps down."

"Yeah. That's the point of uncertainty."

"Huh. How about that."

"Yep," she shrugs.

"That still doesn't explain why we're here, though," I say. "If it doesn't matter either way, I mean."

Rachida sighs. "Times like this, the best thing we can do is just record the events in front of us."

The sun begins to dip below the horizon. Each wave that laps against the bank of the river brings with it a flash of orange light. For a moment, the serenity of our environment overtakes everything else.

"I've been thinking."

I look over at her.

"Mm?"

"Just... what we're doing. Living outside it all. Basically looking out for this lot. It's..."

"What?"

"It's not... the worst way we could be spending our time." I burst out laughing. "Oh, shut up. You know what I mean." I nod, still grinning. "I'm just starting to think I could get used to this."

"Me too."

She reaches over, her hand outstretched. I take it.

We sit and watch the day turn to night.

ACKNOWLEDGMENTS

Arden Fraser, Ele Reynolds, and Casey Morell, for editing the manuscript of this book.

China Miéville, Douglas Adams, William S. Burroughs, Will Self and Chuck Palahniuk for being the sort of writers that I can only ever hope to rival.

Advice For Strays, by Justine Kilkerr, and *Gone Home*, by The Fullbright Company, for making things that motivated me to make more stuff and to do it well.

ABOUT THE AUTHOR

Christopher J. Fraser is a writer living in Massachusetts. He has written one other collection of short fiction, *Tales From the End*, and is a regular contributor to the film magazine *Bright Wall/Dark Room*.

Head to dystopolis.tumblr.com and type the password "cainlives" for a free digital copy of this book!